"I'm A Very Uncomplicated Man."

"Any man who has an agent, enough money in the bank to pay the national debt and scads of adoring fans is not uncomplicated."

"Okay," he said, laughing, "I'm as uncomplicated as my situation will permit. And right now I'm thinking some very uncomplicated thoughts, such as what it will be like to kiss you when I bring you home."

"I told you, I don't go out with baseball players, and that includes kissing them. I really don't want to see you."

"I don't believe you." Ryan smiled.

Dallas smiled back. "That's because I'm lying."

Dear Reader,

Welcome to Silhouette! Our goal is to give you hours of unbeatable reading pleasure, and we hope you'll enjoy each month's six new Silhouette Desires. These sensual, provocative love stories are both believable and compelling—sometimes they're poignant, sometimes humorous, but always enjoyable.

Indulge yourself. Experience all the passion and excitement of falling in love along with our heroine as she meets the irresistible man of her dreams and together they overcome all obstacles in the path to a happy ending.

If this is your first Desire, I hope it'll be the first of many. If you're already a Silhouette Desire reader, thanks for your support! Look for some of your favorite authors in the coming months: Stephanie James, Diana Palmer, Dixie Browning, Ann Major and Doreen Owens Malek, to name just a few.

Happy reading!

Isabel Swift
Senior Editor

MARIE NICOLE
Foxy Lady

Silhouette Desire

Published by Silhouette Books New York

America's Publisher of Contemporary Romance

SILHOUETTE BOOKS
300 East 42nd St., New York, N.Y. 10017

ISBN: 0-373-05315-0

First Silhouette Books printing November 1986

America's Publisher of Contemporary Romance

Books by Marie Nicole

Silhouette Desire

Tried and True #112
Buyer Beware #142
Through Laughter and Tears #161
Grand Theft: Heart #182
A Woman of Integrity #197
Country Blue #224
Last Year's Hunk #274
Foxy Lady #315

Silhouette Romance

Man Undercover #373
Please Stand By #394
Mine By Write #411
Getting Physical #440

MARIE NICOLE

is a natural writer because her own life has been so romantic. She met her husband-to-be in tenth grade and began dating him in college. The first time he kissed her he made the room fade away, and things have only gotten better for them since.

To Lucy Tscherne,
for all the quiet, shared moments

One

Hi ya, good-lookin'," Rusty Sullivan called, a low appreciative whistle accompanying the words.

Dallas Carlyle swung around from the outer entrance of the California Rebels' locker room, her shoulder-length sable hair caressing her cheek and framing what others had remarked upon as an incredibly enticing face. Her expression, ever-so-slightly wary, relaxed to one of amusement and recognition. She stepped aside to let one of the team members walk by.

The player gave her an interested look, then nodded at Rusty and hurried off.

Rusty slipped an arm around Dallas's shoulders, pulling her toward him. It was a friendly gesture and nothing more, but he had to admit that Champion Carlyle's little girl had certainly grown up to be something else.

"Looking for me?" he asked suggestively. He backed several steps away from her and held her arms outstretched as he nodded in obvious appreciation of the woman who stood in front of him.

He just didn't have it in him to look lecherous, Dallas thought. He couldn't even do a good job of pretending. "No." She laughed.

Two more players walked out of the locker room. They both stopped talking for an instant as they appraised Dallas. Their approval could be seen in their eyes.

Rusty snapped his fingers, feigning disappointment. He let go of Dallas. "Can't seem to get to first base these days."

"I hadn't noticed," she said innocently.

"That's my girl," he said laughing.

"What're you doing here?"

"I've been assigned to cover the Rebels." She was pleased with the arrangement. After all, the Rebels had been her dad's team, and she had a lot of good memories of those days.

"Hey, no kidding!"

"No kidding," she echoed. "Do me a favor, Rusty?"

"For you, babe, anything."

"Tell Ryan Fox that I'd like to see him."

"Oh, not you, too, Dallas," Rusty moaned.

She looked at him, puzzled. "What's that supposed to mean?"

"Ever since he got here this season none of us guys has been able to get to first base with the ladies," he complained. "They all want to see The Fox."

The Fox. The nickname made her think of a predator. From what Arnold had enviously reported when he'd covered the team for the newspaper before her, her interpretation of the name fit. It was a wonder Fox found any time at all for baseball. She had seen his picture in the papers often enough to surmise that he traded women faster than he traded teams. How did he manage his swinging life and still make it in by curfew?

"This, I assure you, is strictly business. And might I remind you that most of you 'boys' have wives waiting for you back home?" She smiled, knowing full well that Rusty's philandering was restricted to the exercise of a good imagination.

Rusty rolled his eyes. "Don't I know it. Five feet of dangerous curves and mean disposition."

"I'll share that little description with Laura the next time I run into her," Dallas promised. She tucked the worn clipboard under her arm. It had been her father's when he had this route. Now it was hers.

"Now, Dallas, you wouldn't do that to a friend of your daddy's, would you?" he asked, cozying up to her. "After all, I gave you your first interview."

"Yes," Dallas said, smiling, "you did. And you're never going to let me forget that, are you?"

His gray eyes sparkled. "Uh-uh."

Rusty Sullivan was the "old man" of the team, nearly forty years old and still going strong. Dallas knew for a fact that he used bottled help to retain his deep chestnut-colored hair. But he needed no help to remain the youthful, puckish man she had always known. When she was twelve she had a crush on him that had been so overwhelming she had thought she would die from it. He and her father had been friends since the days when her father played professional baseball. They had "acquired" Rusty, now that she thought of it, the same summer her mother had left. Rusty had always managed to drop by when he was in town. These days she felt as comfortable with Rusty as she would have with a pair of old slippers.

Dallas grinned. She knew Rusty liked to think of himself as quite the ladies' man, despite his fifteen-year marriage to Laura. He didn't exactly see himself in the same category as an old pair of slippers.

That was the difference, Dallas thought, between Rusty and the new breed of athletes. Rusty had self-esteem; the others had egos. Monumental egos. Because of the adulation they received, many of them felt they could do anything they wanted to and had a right to command a king's ransom as payment for their talents.

Ryan T. Fox fell into that classification. This was quite a different show from the days when her father had been third-baseman for the Rebels, or even from the days later on when he had been a sports writer assigned to the team. Dallas didn't look forward to interviewing Fox. She found herself bored with the new cocky athletes. She was more at home with the veterans. Maybe, she mused, that was why she was experiencing an itch to branch out, to do something else besides just follow sports. Sports weren't what they used to be.

Fox was the current golden boy of baseball. He possessed a pitching arm that most pitchers would have sold their souls for. He could do everything with a baseball but make it waltz. Still, the millions of dollars guaranteed in his contract seemed utterly ludicrous, Dallas thought. Nobody was worth that kind of money.

"Send him out here to me when he's dressed, okay?" she asked Rusty.

"That's a first." Rusty chuckled mischievously. "Most of the ladies who ask for him usually leave out the last part."

"Just send him out," she prodded.

Rusty gave her a little bow, swung open the door and disappeared into the locker room.

A pungent odor consisting of sweat, dampness, rubbing alcohol and a variety of men's colognes permeated the locker area. It was still half full. Rusty passed several of his teammates in different stages of dress. Richard Culhane still sat on the bench he had occupied for the last half hour, a gray-white towel draped haphazardly about his hips as he pondered a crossword puzzle. It was his way of unwinding. He caught sight of Rusty out of the corner of his eye.

"Hey, Sullivan, what's a ten letter word for—"

"I dunno," Rusty answered mechanically before Culhane had finished his question. Rusty's command of the English language was not of the highest caliber, and spelling was something he left to others.

"Hey, Foxy," he called out, rounding a corner.

A tall, broad-shouldered man turned and slung a towel over the locker. "I thought you'd left," he said, surprised to see Rusty return.

Ryan reached for his briefs and began pulling them on. The muscles in the backs of his legs tightened as he balanced himself. Rusty looked on enviously for a moment, wishing that his mirror reflected that kind of image. Every inch of Ryan Fox was a symphony of muscles and sinews.

"I did, but I ran into a sports reporter outside who wants to see you. Name of Dallas Carlyle." He watched Ryan's tanned face for some hint of recognition.

Ryan stood for a moment, his clothes temporarily forgotten. He ran the name through his mind. He had seen it on the byline of a column once, he thought. But it didn't connect with a face. "What's he want?"

Rusty was about to correct him and say that Dallas was a woman, but his love of practical jokes stopped him. "An interview," he said innocently.

"Well," Ryan said, shrugging, "send him on in."

Rusty saluted, suppressing his grin. "Will do."

He chuckled to himself all the way out.

"Well?" Dallas asked when Rusty emerged.

"He wants you to come in."

"But—" she began. She had made it a strict policy never to conduct an interview in the men's locker room. Even though the courts had handed down permission to do so, she had always seen the action as nothing short of an invasion of privacy. She could wait the extra few minutes it took for a player to get his clothes on and come out.

Rusty saw her hesitation. "He insisted." Rusty fought to keep a straight face. "Said that it would be the only way you'd get an interview."

Was he one of those? she wondered. One of those pig-headed chauvinists who thought that a woman's place was next to a warm stove or in a warm bed, not with a hot typewriter at a tie game? Did he think he would scare her away with his challenge? Dallas set her mouth.

"Well, if that's the way it has to be," she muttered, pushing against the door, "that's the way it has to be." Nothing annoyed her more than sexism. She'd seen more than her share of it. After being raised by her father as a real tomboy, she was both dazed and upset to find that everyone else didn't look at her in the same unbiased light.

Rusty jumped out of her way and innocently strode behind her, waiting to see the fun.

For one moment Dallas hesitated outside the actual locker room door. She glanced at Rusty's face and saw his amused expression. Then she squared her shoulders, pushed open the last barrier and walked in.

"Anyone know a thirteen-letter word for someone combining the characteristics of both sexes?" Culhane called out.

Dallas glanced at the man's attire, or lack of it and raised her eyes, trying to maintain an indifferent expression. Keep your cool, Carlyle, or you're sunk, she told herself.

"Hermaphrodite," she answered, staring straight ahead as she continued walking.

Culhane was about to thank her and then gaped, staring after her swaying figure.

Rusty winked at Culhane and mouthed the words, "Hands off," to his teammate.

"Which way?" she asked Rusty, wanting to get this over with, even if she was partially to blame for her own embarrassment. After all, she was the one who had convinced her editor to run a feature on a prominent figure in baseball in the Sunday magazine instead of the sports section. It was her stab at branching out, at showing Darcy Ames that she was capable of doing something other than just reporting scores and errors. Darcy had been the one to pick the player. Dallas would have been a lot happier interviewing Rusty.

Damn Fox, why couldn't he display some manners and opt to meet her outside?

"There he is." Rusty gestured toward the end of the locker row. "In the flesh."

"I'll say," Dallas muttered.

Ryan was just reaching for his shirt. Firm pectorals rippled invitingly as he pulled it on. Dallas made a quick assessment. He stood about five ten, she guessed. High-heeled cowboy boots stood next to his bare feet. Boots and a weather-beaten Stetson contributed to his image of being the backwoods boy who had made good—both on the field and off.

She could see how he might cause a woman's pulse to race. He was handsome, all right, in a breathstopping sort of way. There was far more to him than any photo could capture.

"Someone here to see you, Foxy," Rusty called out.

Ryan turned, his hand out, ready to greet the writer Rusty had brought in. The friendly gesture was halted abruptly, just before he made contact with Dallas's hand. It was clear that he was surprised to see a woman. The soft expression in his eyes hardened slightly.

"This is Dallas Carlyle," Rusty went on. "The sports writer I told you about."

Dallas reached for Ryan's hand and shook it. At least one of them was going to have manners, she thought.

"A sports writer?" Ryan's hand dropped to his side.

She could see that he disapproved of her choice of vocation. Well, that was fine. She disapproved of arrogant players who jumped from team to team without an iota of loyalty and commanded exorbitant salaries along the way.

"That's what the man said when he hired me," she answered, a tight smile on her face.

He studied her for a moment without saying anything. "Like walking into men's locker rooms, do you?" he asked archly.

She felt her defensiveness growing. A chauvinist, just as she had thought. An overpaid, swollen-headed chauvinist who thought he was qualified to pass judgment on everyone else just because the owner of the Rebels had rocks in his head and had signed him to a contract that could have made up the annual budget of a small South American country. "Not particularly," she answered evenly.

"Then why are you standing here?" It was clear that he didn't believe her answer.

Ryan buttoned his shirt slowly. Normally he wasn't rude, but Ryan didn't like pushy women. The two female sports writers he had run into previously had soured his taste for the breed. And of late aggressive women were the only kind he met. For the past two years he had been subjected to a bevy of women who clamored for his attention and entrance to his bed. The principled, three-dimensional women he had known while he was growing up were sorely lacking in this new high-powered world he found himself in.

While he loved the game of baseball and normally enjoyed the camaraderie of the other team members, he was disappointed with the type of women the game attracted. And pushy female sports reporters and sportscasters were at the head of his complaint list.

What was wrong with the man? Dallas wondered. First he asked her into the locker room, then he insulted her for being there. "Look, I'm here by invitation," she reminded him pointedly.

"Oh." She had stumped him for a moment, and he looked accusingly at Rusty.

"Hey," Rusty said quickly, stepping between them. His joke was clearly backfiring. "Why don't we all get together over a drink at The Well and see what the lady has to say?" he suggested to Ryan.

"The lady has to say that she has a deadline and a limited amount of time to waste on game playing. The sooner we get this started the sooner we'll both be happy."

She had pepper, Ryan decided. He would give her that. He found that there was something exceedingly attractive about the pugnacious way she raised her chin. "Sounds good to me," he said. This time, there was no animosity in his voice. He liked the fire that entered her green eyes, and the way she tossed her hair. What color was that, anyway? It made him think of chinchillas curled up against one another on a lazy winter day.

"Fine, then it's settled. The Well in ten minutes?" Rusty asked Dallas.

Dallas nodded. Might as well, she thought. She felt as if she were going to need a drink in order to face this arrogant pitcher. God's gift to the slider, as well as to women, she added sarcastically. At least that was probably what he thought. She had been involved with

the game practically all of her life, and she had seen
players come and go. Mr. Ryan T. Fox was in for a
rude surprise if he thought he was unique or irre-
placeable. She turned and walked out.

"Hey, Dallas," a voice called from the back of the
room, "how about interviewing me?"

Another woman might have just kept on walking,
put off by the leer in the man's voice. But Dallas had
grown up with the peculiar sense of humor that typi-
fied athletes. She turned, casting an eye to the back of
the room. She recognized the man. A slow smile took
hold. "Sorry, McGee, you only rate a line this time
around," she teased. "Maybe later."

Allan McGee laughed. "Wait till next year," he
called after her.

"That's what they all say," she said and laughed as
she walked out, the doors swinging shut behind her.

"He know her?" Ryan asked Rusty, nodding toward McGee.

"Sure. So do I, and so do a bunch of the other
guys."

Ryan absently wondered just how well they knew
the stunning woman and how far she would go to get
a good story.

"Hey, get that expression off your face," Rusty
warned. "It's not what you think. She's not like that."

Rusty's sudden protectiveness interested Ryan. "She
walked in here, didn't she?"

"That was my fault," Rusty admitted, waiting for
Ryan to collect his belongings.

Ryan shut his locker and glanced at Rusty. "You dragged her in?"

"No, but I told her that you wouldn't give her an interview any other way." Ryan looked at him, mildly confused. "Just my idea of livening things up a little." Rusty shrugged good-naturedly. "Take it from me, Dallas is okay."

Ryan began to walk out. "Define 'okay,'" he threw over his shoulder as he waited for Rusty to follow him.

"A good egg."

The definition fell short in Ryan's estimation. "She makes me think more of an omelet. Something warm to be served at breakfast."

Rusty caught the easy, sensuous smile on Ryan's lips. He felt himself growing protective. He had known Dallas since her silhouette was straight. "Uh-uh, Dallas isn't that kind of girl."

Ryan put his arm around Rusty's shoulder as they walked down the long, dim corridor. "Okay, tell me just what kind of 'girl' she is, although if anyone ever deserved the title 'woman,' it's her."

"I know what you mean," Rusty agreed. "But you should have seen her as a kid. Most of the time she was too busy trying to be a boy."

Rusty lost him. "Come again?"

"Her old man was C. C. Carlyle."

Ryan stopped walking for a moment, his expression incredulous. "Champion Carlyle, the third-baseman?"

"One and the same," Rusty told him, nodding solemnly.

"Hey, his column ran in the newspaper back home." For a moment Ryan was a kid again, riffling through the paper quickly to read the column before his father chased him outdoors. "I used to read it before feeding the chickens."

"Feeding chickens?" Rusty echoed with a laugh. He scratched his head. "I knew there was something seedy about you."

"That's 'wholesome,'" Ryan corrected good-naturedly.

Rusty let loose with a loud laugh. "You and the word wholesome don't belong in the same conversation."

Ryan smiled easily. "A lot you know."

"Look, boy, you've been with us for less than a season and already there's a line of girls—"

"Women."

"Whatever, as long as an ape's arm ready to follow you around."

"Very poetic."

They came to a halt before the outer door. "It's very *something*," Rusty said wistfully. "How do you do it?"

"Very simple. I tell them all the truth."

That didn't sound right. "Which truth?"

"The only one that counts, that I won't get married." Ryan shook his head, as if somewhat mystified by it all. "Nothing seems to goad a woman on, more than a challenge."

Rusty frowned glumly as he turned to the door. "I can't use that line. I'm already married."

"It's not a line," Ryan said, heading outside to the field. "I don't intend to get married. Never met a woman yet who made me want to settle down. Corny as it sounds, I'm looking for the old-fashioned type."

"Barefoot and pregnant?" Rusty guessed.

Ryan laughed. "Old-fashioned, Sullivan, not archaic. I'm looking for a woman who's loyal. Someone who wants kids, someone who's willing to put up with a bit of bad temper at times. Someone with a little depth."

"Oh, Ryan," a buxom woman called, waving at him from the sidelines.

Rusty glanced at the woman's expansive upper silhouette. "I dunno, that seems like enough depth to me."

"Does your wife know you're drooling?"

"My wife thinks I live the life of a monk when I'm away, and I don't tell her any different."

Ryan smiled. He knew a lot of players who led dual lives, burning the candle at both ends, but Rusty wasn't one of them, although he talked a good game and liked to flirt whenever he could. That was why, Ryan thought, he had wound up being friends with the man. Although he made no comment to the contrary, deep down Ryan didn't approve of married men who fooled around. You either made a commitment, or you didn't. You didn't play it both ways. It was as simple as that.

A swarm of people, young and old, converged on the two players as they tried to make their way out of the ball park. Baseballs, books and scraps of paper were thrust in their direction by eager hands.

"Ryan, Ryan, sign mine."

"Sign mine."

A definite chant went up. A few fans were interested enough to approach Rusty first, feeling that they might as well get something while they were waiting. Rusty took it all philosophically.

"Hey, Ryan, Dallas is waiting," Rusty reminded him as the crowd around them grew.

Ryan made no move to leave. He took another baseball, this one slightly grimy. He looked for a clean space to sign for the enraptured-looking twelve-year-old who had handed it to him.

"Let her wait," Ryan said easily. "This is more important." He grinned at the boy, who looked as if he had died and gone to heaven now that he had actually made contact with his idol.

Dallas looked at her watch. Five o'clock. It was exactly one hour since she had been in Ryan Fox's company. It didn't take an hour to button your shirt no matter how much you puffed up your chest, she thought, annoyed. It also didn't take an hour to get to the small restaurant from the stadium. She had made it in five minutes.

She pressed her lips together. She was being stood up. She took a sip of the Kahlua and cream she had been nursing since she had gotten there and tasted predominantly melted ice. She let the tiny umbrella she was twirling drop from her fingers.

Enough was enough.

If Ryan T. Fox didn't want to talk to her, she could damn well tell Darcy he had to come up with a player who wasn't so full of himself. *T* for The, huh? More like The Weasel than The Fox. It took more than looks to make it in Dallas's book. It took manners, integrity and a bit of moral fiber. And it seemed that Mr. Ryan T. Fox, she thought as she slid her purse off the table, possessed none of the above.

Dallas stood up, not unmindful that as she did so a stranger across the bar looked hopefully her way. One encouraging movement from her and she knew she would have him at her side. Dallas did her best to pretend that she saw someone in the distance. That was all she needed right now, she thought, some half-inebriated lothario trying to make points with her.

She moved past a small table of players. After a home game this was their favorite hangout. The mood was boisterous tonight. After all, they had won, and things looked pretty good for a shot at the pennant. Ryan had pitched a great game.

Probably true on and off the field, Dallas thought, annoyed at having been treated so cavalierly. She wasn't used to it. Her position on the *L.A. News* generally garnered her a great deal of respect, and her looks attracted men like the proverbial flies. She had never been stood up before.

"Hi, Dallas, how's it going?" a Rebel player called out.

"Not as good as it is for you," she answered, catching a glimpse of a familiar face.

The face brought with it a name and a batting average simultaneously. It was training her father had instilled in her. It was all he had given her, besides a great deal of love, and it had been enough.

"Looks like you've got a pretty good shot at the pennant from where I stand, Jawersky," she added.

The player she was addressing, as well as the others at his table, broke into a chorus of agreement. "Just five games away," the third-baseman said proudly. The man on his left bobbed his head up and down as he looked at Dallas.

"Don't get too cocky, Jawersky," Dallas warned playfully. "You're not there yet."

"No, but we will be."

Dallas turned toward the voice behind her and found herself looking up into Ryan Fox's dark blue eyes.

Two

Well," Ryan said, his tone clearly indicating that he had resigned himself to the situation the way a child reluctantly accepts medicine, "shall we see about getting a table?" He looked at her expectantly.

Dallas didn't like his tone, and she had no qualms about showing her displeasure. "I've *had* a table for one hour and—" she glanced at her watch "—five minutes."

Feisty, aren't you? he thought. Ryan gave her an easy smile. He seemed to instinctively know that it would goad her. "Patience is a virtue." He spoke the words slowly as if to accentuate his point.

"So is punctuality," she countered without hesitation.

Rusty placed himself between them. "We ran into some fans," he told Dallas quickly. He didn't understand just what was going on here, but he had the definite impression that he could very well get wounded in the cross fire if he didn't do something *now*. He wondered if his harmless little joke in the locker room was to blame for this antagonism. No, there was too much electricity in the air for that. This was something of their own making.

"And you left them for me?" Dallas asked Ryan, her wide-eyed expression adding to the sarcasm in her voice. "I'm flattered."

"You ought to be, lady." Ryan took hold of her arm as he guided her to a just-vacated table. "I don't generally give interviews." And he wasn't exactly sure why he was giving one now, except that perhaps it had something to do with the fact that she was C. C. Carlyle's daughter and represented a tie to his past. That, and the fact that there was something about her that intrigued him. He had noted it in the locker room and again just now.

Dallas managed to extricate herself from his grasp. "You don't have to hang on to me," she informed him tersely. "I'm not some pop fly you caught in the bottom of the ninth."

"I'd say you're nothing like a pop fly." Ryan straddled a seat comfortably and nodded at the chair next to him. "Pop flies are easy to handle."

"I don't 'handle' at all," she told him coolly.

She was becoming more interesting by the moment. She was fiery, feisty and good-looking, and the sum total made her extremely sexy.

If you're going to get anywhere with this interview, you're going to have to strike some kind of truce, she schooled herself. Maybe she needed a few seconds to regain her composure. She took a seat and pretended to search for something in her shoulder bag.

She knew she was overreacting and yet, for some reason, she couldn't help herself. Ryan Fox's presence brought out—no, *demanded*—some sort of reaction from her, from everyone. He wasn't the type of person who just blended in with the furniture, or whose presence could be taken for granted. She could see why women felt compelled to respond to him. And from his reputation and what Arnold had told her when he gave her the pitcher's background, Fox had encountered more than his share of bright, smiling, round-heeled groupies dying to get their turn at bat.

To Dallas's surprise Ryan leaned forward and looked straight into her eyes. "Anyone ever try?"

"Try what?" Her mouth felt unexpectedly dry.

"To handle you."

"How about a drink?" Rusty interjected brightly, attempting to dispel the growing tension. He knew Dallas. She was straightforward and very professional. He felt an explosion building. "I could sure use one." He cleared his throat rather dramatically, searching for something to say. "Nothing like a baseball game to make me parched."

Ryan glanced at Rusty and noticed that the man was giving him a warning look. He leaned back in his chair. "What's the problem?"

The din in the room came in waves. It was at its crest at the moment, and Rusty used the noise as a shield. "She's got a hell of a temper," he said to Ryan. "I wouldn't try pushing her."

Ryan merely grinned. "Thanks for the advice."

Rusty immediately regretted his comment. He had a feeling that Ryan would take it as a challenge.

Fox was grinning. What was he grinning about? Dallas wondered. The room was dimly lit, but it didn't take floodlights to let her see that a gleam had entered his eyes. She could see it even beneath the broad brim of his tan Stetson.

And then the gleam faded. Ryan said something to Rusty that she couldn't quite make out. Her mind drifted into a corner where she always retreated to sort things out, or just to observe. Right now the clamor was giving her an opportunity to observe Ryan. As far as looks went, she had already seen what all the excitement was about. He had a sensual, sensitive face, yet it seemed oddly compatible with his muscular physique. The pale-blue shirt he wore was rolled up at the sleeves and called attention to his forearms. Forearms made hard, she surmised, by hours of pitching. She could see the veins standing out along the bulge of the muscle. For a fraction of a second she felt an urge to reach out and run her fingers along his arm just to reassure herself that it was warm and that he was a flesh-and-blood man, not some mythical "Casey at the bat."

"Why don't you see about those drinks?" Ryan suggested to Rusty.

Rusty rose. He looked uncertainly from one to another. "What'll you have?"

"The usual," Ryan said, his eyes never leaving Dallas.

She felt them burning through the warm, sultry haze generated by too many bodies packed in too little space. "Beer," she told Rusty when he looked toward her.

"Three beers coming up." His voice was cheerful. "If I hear any loud explosions I won't bother coming back."

"Want to start over again?" Ryan asked as Rusty began weaving through the barricade of bodies between their table and the bar.

Dallas shrugged noncommittally, pretending that she didn't understand him. "Fine by me, I guess."

He leaned back in his chair, still studying her. He tucked his thumb under the brim of his hat and pushed it high on the crown of his head. "You're not going to get anywhere by riding on your high horse, lady. I know what I've got against female reporters." He saw Dallas set her jaw. "But why don't you tell me what you've got against me?"

She met his gaze and held it, willing him to look away. It turned out to be her first mistake. There was something almost paralyzing about his eyes. They were smiling broadly. Was he laughing at her? Perhaps he was just trying to be friendly—or on the make. The one thing she did know was that she had never seen eyes so incredibly blue before. "What makes you think I have something against you?" she asked slowly.

He grinned again, and Dallas found it quite engaging. She was reminded about the legend of Davy Crockett grinning down a b'ar. "Call it instinct. I'm a farm boy—"

"Yes, I know." The idea struck her as humorous.

He tried to ignore her tone. "And I learned to go by my instincts early on. What's so funny?" he finally couldn't help asking.

"You'll forgive me, but I don't quite picture you as Gary Cooper, kicking the dirt with the toe of your boot and saying 'Aw shucks.'"

"Okay—" he spread his hands wide "—what do you picture me as?"

There were all sorts of tactful things to say at such a moment, but Dallas didn't feel like being tactful. Not after having been made to wait over an hour. Instead she blurted out what was really on her mind. Harsh as it was, something within her told her that Ryan would appreciate the truth. "A philanderer. A womanizer. Someone with no loyalty."

"All this in five minutes?"

Rather than angry, she saw that he was amused. Dallas drew herself up, her chin jutting out a little. She didn't like being laughed at.

It was a sharp chin, Ryan thought, studying her. An aggressive chin. It suggested to him that she liked to argue—and to win.

"No, the last five minutes only confirmed what I've heard and read in any number of articles," she said curtly.

He felt justified in his original feelings toward the female members of her profession. "Now you know why I don't give interviews. You ladies and gentlemen of the press put people down whenever it suits you. Or perhaps," he added, looking at her keenly, "you write whatever you think will sell."

"Oh? Then you're not getting an astronomically high salary?" she asked innocently.

"Yes, but—"

"And you haven't switched teams three times in three years?"

"That's a matter of record." He felt his patience slipping.

"And you haven't been seen with a score of women on your arm?"

"Not at the same time."

"No, even you wouldn't have an ego that large," she muttered audibly.

What *was* it about this man that goaded her on like this? she wondered. She had interviewed prima donnas before, some far less polite than Ryan. There had been one who had propositioned her right after she introduced herself. She had dealt with him quite professionally. She had never reacted this way before.

It made her feel unsure of herself for the first time since her father had died, and she resented Ryan for it.

"I think I came back just in time." Beer sloshed over the tops of the glasses and onto the table as Rusty set down the three tankards. "The static electricity around this table is making the hair on my arms stand up." The grin he wore was extra wide in hopes of quelling whatever it was that he had just walked in on.

Ryan eased himself back in his chair again. "Miss Carlyle has found a new way to conduct an interview—browbeating the subject to death."

"You seem none the worse for it," she said crisply, attempting to hide her chagrin. She had overstepped her bounds. She had never let her own feelings, good or bad, get in the way of an interview. Yet here she sat, amid smoke and noise, attacking a man she knew only by reputation. She wasn't even sure why she was doing it except that somehow she felt oddly threatened by him. What she did know was that she wasn't being fair.

Rusty knew it, too. She could tell by the look in his eyes.

"I've got good reflexes," Ryan answered her. He took a sip of his beer, then gave Dallas another long, penetrating look. "So, do you want to continue this thing or not?"

There was something in the way he said it, something in the way he looked at her, that told Dallas there was a lot more than an interview going on here.

You're being ridiculous, she told herself. You're letting the man's press get to you. No, it wasn't the man's press. It was the man. Crowded, noisy bar notwithstanding, Ryan Fox was tapping out a message to her nervous system, and her feminine antennae were picking up the signal.

She lowered her eyes and stared at the lip of the tankard, then took a long drink. "Let's get on with the interview." The beer seemed particularly bitter and helped to bring things back into perspective. "You were born in Laredo, Texas—"

"Kansas City, Missouri," Ryan corrected, taking particular enjoyment in the fact that she had made a mistake.

How had she gotten that wrong? "I thought—"

"I *grew up* in Laredo," he told her before she had a chance to finish her statement. "Trust me. I know where I was born."

His smile annoyed her. "Probably assisted at the birth, no doubt," she murmured under her breath, just loud enough for him to hear. "Okay. Kansas City. How did you get started playing baseball?"

"I don't know," he said quite honestly. She could feel some of his natural charm coming through as he became comfortable. "I just remember always playing it whenever there was a free second on the farm."

"Not a ranch?" Another blunder, she thought, irritated. She had looked to Arnold for a quick thumbnail bio. The vague thought that perhaps some of the other details that Arnold had given her might not be correct either crossed her mind.

"Not a ranch," he said succinctly. "A farm. A dirt farm." His voice lowered so that she had to lean forward to catch the rest of his statement. He appeared to be talking to himself for a moment. "Its only true crop was hopelessness."

"And a prodigy," she put in.

He couldn't tell if she was being sarcastic or not. But he did know at that instant that he was going to find out what made Champion Carlyle's daughter tick if it was the last thing he did. He could feel a latent excitement beginning to travel through his veins just the way it did toward the end of a tie game when the pressure was on and it was all up to him.

"Not a prodigy, just a determined pitcher. I don't like dirt . . . of any variety."

She acknowledged his meaning with a nod. "Is that what makes Ryan run?"

He took another drink before he asked, "Come again?"

"Is fear of poverty what makes you go from team to team?" she asked coolly, thinking back to the days when her father played professional ball. He had stayed with one team until he left the game.

"Forgive me if I ask, but have you got an ax to grind with me?"

"Not you in particular."

"Me in a crowd?" he suggested humorously.

She didn't like the way he seemed to be laughing at her. "I set a high priority on loyalty."

"So do I."

"So why aren't you?"

"The nature of the game has changed since you tagged along behind your dad," he said matter-of-factly.

"Not for the better, as far as I can see," she countered. "There seems to be something lacking when you think that for every player out there on the field, there's an agent in the wings, calculating future moves. Where's the team spirit if everyone is constantly thinking of the most advantageous trade they can make?"

"Owners being what they are, players have to watch out for themselves, then think of the team. We're not like regular people."

I'll buy that one, she thought.

"Our careers can be over by the end of the season. A prolonged slump can wipe us off the roster. Why shouldn't we make the best possible deals while we can? The owners are making a fortune on us. There's enough to go around." He leaned forward, grasping her wrist lightly. Dallas felt something warm and electric leaping along her skin, and she made no move to pull her hand away. "Make no mistake about this, once I'm on a team, once I'm committed, I give it my all, not fifty, not seventy, not ninety-eight percent. My all. They get exactly what they pay for."

Let go of my wrist, she thought. She didn't want to make a scene by struggling to free herself. She wasn't all that sure she *could* struggle. "There are some things money can't buy."

He released her casually. "They get those, too, if they earn them."

She stopped for a moment, feeling she was getting far more than she had initially bargained for. And then she continued. "And just what does a seven-figure contract earn them?"

He could tell she disapproved of his salary. He would have to be an idiot to miss it, he thought. She probably had a lot of fond memories of the camaraderie between players that had existed in her father's day. Undoubtedly her memories were misted over with the romance produced by the past.

"They get the best damn pitcher in the National League."

"Spoken modestly."

The smile that curved her lips tempted him in a way that he hadn't felt tempted in a long, long time.

"Spoken honestly for the present," he responded.

"For the present?" She arched one brow, both amused and amazed that he would speak of mortality.

"There's always someone better waiting to break every record. But right now I'm top gun."

"Yes, ma'am, he is that," Rusty chimed in, nodding in confirmation. He wasn't sure whether to be amused or alarmed. If this had been any woman other than Champion Carlyle's daughter, he would have been amused; he was enjoying seeing Ryan pitted for the first time against a woman who could hold her own. The women he usually saw flocking to Ryan looked as if they could be poured into a cup like warm cocoa at the right word. But because Dallas was Champ's daughter, Rusty felt a personal stake in what was going on.

"Your beer's getting warm," Rusty prodded.

"Don't mother me, Rusty," Dallas said, never shifting her eyes from Ryan.

Rusty drew himself up. "Mother?" he sputtered. "Me?"

Dallas turned to look at him, the tense moment broken. "Sorry, I forgot who I was speaking to. The team Romeo." Her eyes danced as she spoke.

Ryan made a mental note to ask Rusty more about Dallas when he got a chance—soon. He glanced down at the notepad beneath her long, pink-polished nails. "Doesn't look like you've got much so far."

She was tempted to say that perhaps her subject didn't have much to offer, but she knew that wasn't true. She wasn't going to get anywhere by being so antagonistic. What was the matter with her? she wondered again.

"No, I don't," she agreed. "Care to tell me some revealing facts?"

The smile he gave her swamped her senses.

"Not here," he told her.

For a moment, just for a moment, she felt a very warm sensation that zoomed through her veins and disappeared as quickly as it had arisen. "I'm afraid 'here' is where it's going to have to be. I've got a deadline." The deadline was actually at least a week away. Darcy hadn't scheduled the feature to be run for at least two weeks, perhaps three. But she wanted to get this interview over with in one session.

"Why don't you postpone it?" he suggested. "Right now I have the feeling that I wouldn't come off well in anything you wrote."

She lifted her chin defensively, as if she had been found out. She considered his words an affront to her professionalism, though she had to admit they were justified. "What makes you say that?"

"Well, for one thing, you keep scowling at the guy," Rusty pointed out, reaching deeply into a bowl of peanuts.

"I'm not scowling," she retorted. "It's the smoke in here. It makes me squint. And I'd get my hand out of there if I were you. Too many peanuts are going to slow you down."

"What, ruin this body?" Rusty puffed up his chest in mock indignation. "Never. What would my adoring fans say?"

"*She'd* say, 'Lay off the salt, Rusty,'" Dallas said, doing a fair imitation of Rusty's wife.

"Hey, you sound just like Laura," he said in surprise.

"Do you do many imitations?" Ryan asked.

There it was again, that low voice getting to her. What was it about him that got under her skin? she wondered. Rusty had her relaxing, and then one word out of Fox's mouth and she felt . . . strange. That was the only way to describe it. Strange, uncomposed, unsettled. Confused summed it up, she decided.

She stared at Ryan. He had the tan of a California beach boy, the same easy, knowing stance, the same thick, luscious hair worn with styled carelessness, except that his was a little darker, more a dirty blond tending toward brown. But there was more. That ostensible openness was hiding something. He wasn't the "good ol' farm boy," but was he strictly a lothario? And why did she want to know so much? She had always been satisfied to get to know her subjects well enough to do a convincing column. She had never wondered about the players on a personal level before.

She looked down at the silver band on her right hand, a gift from her father. "We're interviewing you, not me. I'll ask the questions, thank you."

Ryan looked at Rusty. "Are you sure her father was C. C. Carlyle and not some master sergeant in the marines?"

At the mention of her father's name a slow, fond smile spread across Dallas's lips. "He could be both when he had to be. Now that's the last of your questions. I'm running late. Let's do mine."

Ryan gestured grandly. "Ask away."

For the next twenty minutes Dallas did her best to keep a professional distance between herself and her subject. She asked Ryan questions in such rapid succession that he felt he was under siege, and some of her questions were so slanted that he knew she wasn't really hearing anything he had to say.

Finally he put his hand over hers as she scribbled down still another note. "Why don't you just fill in all the blanks for me?" Smoldering green eyes looked up into his. "I mean, you've got preconceived notions and you don't seem to want to pay attention to any of my answers."

Before Dallas could answer there was a very loud squeal behind her. She turned her head just in time to see them descend. There were three of them. Three women in some of the tightest clothing she had ever seen. The blonde in front elbowed Dallas aside without so much as a glance in her direction, her gaudily wrapped torso blocking Dallas's access to her beer. The other two women vied for space on Ryan's left.

"Are you somebody?" one of the women asked Rusty.

"He is to his wife," Dallas quipped, attempting to rise. The woman in front of her made no move to step aside. She didn't seem to take any notice at all of anything in the room except Ryan.

"Mr. Fox, will you give me your autograph?" she gushed.

Ryan looked around for a piece of paper or something that would pass for an autograph book. "You don't have anything to sign."

"Yes, I do," she gushed, producing a pen. "Right here." She thrust her very ample bustline at him. Scarlet fingernails patted the long, thin collar that framed a plunging neckline.

The man's going to drown in cleavage if he's not careful, Dallas thought, executing a mighty thrust with her hip. Jarred, the woman glared at Dallas. It was Dallas's turn to ignore her. "I'll be running along now, Mr. Fox. I see you have your hands full—or will. Rusty, give my love to Laura." She looked back at Ryan. "It's been . . . interesting."

"Is the interview over?" Rusty asked, surprised.

"It is for now." With that she took her purse, her pad and herself out of the immediate area.

That was one hell of a golden boy, Pop, she thought as she let the evening air hit her face. She took a deep breath and walked to her car, her fingers itching to get at the keys of her typewriter. She smiled as she began to frame her article in her mind.

You might have probing navy-blue eyes and 2.0 Earned Run Average, Ryan T. Fox, but you don't rate in my book.

Smiling, she gunned the engine of her blue Toyota, the last gift her father had given her, and drove to the house they had shared until his death.

Three

Ryan bypassed Rusty's cluttered bed, stripped off his shirt and dropped it in a heap on his own mattress. According to the terms of his contract he could have had private accommodations, but he liked Rusty's company, liked the way the other man went on and on when he told a story. Rusty reminded Ryan of the people he had left back home, and reminders of home were important to him. But right now he wasn't thinking of home. He was thinking of flashing green eyes and a mouth that looked too sensuous for its own good. And thick, sable hair that begged to be touched. A woman who begged to be touched.

"Wouldn't she like to hear that." He laughed. If nothing else, she had been honest, honest to a fault. He knew exactly where he stood with her.

Or did he? All the time he had been answering her questions and sparring with her, there had been another level of conversation going on, and it was only now reaching his consciousness. He had had a hint of it when he had stifled an urge to close her mouth in mid-sentence with a kiss.

Maybe he had stood on the mound for one too many sunny days, he thought.

Ryan sat down on the corner of his bed, his arms folded across his chest. He was staring straight ahead, but he wasn't seeing anything. His mind was far away. Only the distant sound of running water registered. Rusty was in the shower, singing something that sounded vaguely like a top ten hit from a dozen years ago.

It was unusual for a woman to occupy Ryan's mind for more than a few moments at a time. This one, he thought, was something else again. She had captured his imagination *and* his attention with her strange, compelling mixture of sensuality, confidence and vulnerability. He had seen her vulnerability in her eyes when her father had been mentioned, and had sensed it when he had touched her hand. He had a feeling that her exterior bravado was just a way of hiding that softer side from the rest of the world.

He smiled to himself as he toyed with a pillow, kneading it against his flat, muscular middle. She certainly didn't sound as if she had any use for him. Well, he had a use for her. He wanted to see her again. More than see her, he wanted to *be* with her again.

And he was damned if he knew why. There were certainly more willing women around. If he had given any encouragement at all to the woman with the plunging decolletage that now sported his signature, she would have been his for the asking for as long as he wanted. But he didn't want something so meaningless, so trivial.

He had been tired of it almost from the first.

Women had never been in short supply for Ryan, not since he had turned thirteen and girls had suddenly noticed his raw, blond good looks. Now that he was a big-league ballplayer he found himself the object of more offers than he knew what to do with.

"Casanova would have died with a smile on his face just trying to fill one third of the offers you've had," Rusty had told him enviously that evening when the trio of baseball Annies had left their table, disappointed that all they could snare from Ryan was his autograph and his smile.

Ryan had merely nodded absently, looking off in the direction Dallas had taken shortly before.

"One class act, huh?" Rusty had said, munching another handful of peanuts. He hadn't missed the way Ryan had looked after Dallas when she had left them.

"What's her story?"

Rusty had stopped chewing. "Come again?"

"Why is she in this business?"

"It's the only thing she knows. Her mother split when she was eight. Couldn't take the long absences. She didn't want to be the good little woman at home anymore, I guess. Champ came home one night to find Dallas huddled in her bed, crying, and a note on the kitchen table. He went through a real dark depression for a while, fell into a slump, the whole bit. He and Dallas became totally dependent on each other.''

Rusty spoke of the incident with the air of someone who had witnessed it all firsthand. ''Were you there?'' Ryan asked.

''I was a rookie at the time. He had taken me under his wing just before it happened. He had a habit of doing that, looking after the new guys. He was on the team for fifteen years before he retired. Never played on any other team. That's where she gets her attitude from, I guess.''

''I guess,'' Ryan repeated, cradling his beer stein between his palms. The head had long since dissolved, and he had lost his taste for it.

''He took her everywhere with him. Even got her a tutor so she could keep up with her school work during the season. He was determined not to let her feel abandoned by both parents. I suppose,'' Rusty mused quietly, ''he was trying to make up for his mistake with Rhonda.''

''Rhonda?''

''His wife.''

''Did he ever hear from her again?''

Rusty had nodded. ''Just once. A Christmas card, saying that she was happy at last and to forgive her if he could.''

"Did he?" Ryan had asked.

"He burned it." Rusty tilted his glass and saw that it was empty. "We'd better be heading back."

Ryan pulled his Stetson forward, his lanky body brushing against the table as he stood up. "Did she stay with him when he took over the sports beat?"

Again Rusty nodded. "Until she headed for college. And then she spent all her summers with him. She helped him cover the games. They were some team," Rusty said fondly as they walked out into the parking lot.

He had quite a shadow to best, Ryan thought now, fluffing up the pillow and resting his chin on it. He had the ghost of Champion Carlyle to vanquish before he could get to first base with Dallas.

Ryan set his mouth firmly. Ghostbusting was in vogue these days. He reached for the phone, hesitated, then put it down as the sound of running water and off-key singing abruptly stopped. A phone call wouldn't be enough.

Dallas rubbed one bare foot against the other, pleased with herself. Under the table, next to her feet, were the high heels she had carelessly cast off. She was wearing her father's old baseball shirt, the one they had retired when he left the team. Number twenty-one. He had given it to her as a joke on her twenty-first birthday, and she had kept it ever since. It was a little frayed now with age, but she loved it. It reminded her of a happier time. In a way, it was a link to her father.

She had changed quickly when she had come home, determined to get at least part of the article down on paper while her impressions were fresh.

As she wrote she intermixed her interview with the highlights of the game, turning the piece into a thinly veiled warning about the fickleness of fame. Today's hero was tomorrow's sacrifice. The article turned into a discussion of how the game of baseball had changed from simple entertainment representing America at its most uncomplicated to something sadly complex. For every man on the field there was now an agent, a publicist and Lord-only-knew-who else waiting to take a piece of the action. Each team member wasn't a player, he was a walking conglomerate. Bring back yesteryear, her article said wistfully in conclusion.

The cuckoo clock in the hall announced that it was eight. She had been writing for two hours. Dallas laced her fingers overhead and stretched from side to side. She was tired and vaguely dissatisfied. The article, at least the rough draft, was done. And yet there was an unfinished quality to it. While it was a good piece, it wasn't what she had set out to write. And, she admitted to herself, there wasn't all that much about Ryan Fox in it.

She rubbed the bridge of her nose. She felt a little under the weather. Maybe she had a cold coming on. That was probably why she had reacted to Ryan the way she had, she decided. Her resistance was down.

People's minds started to wander under the influence of a fever.

She got up and padded across the almond-colored carpet to her kitchen.

"And how are you tonight, Fish?" she asked the lone goldfish in the bowl that stood on her kitchen counter next to an empty cookie jar. A tiny sea green castle with two windows was the only thing in the bowl keeping Fish company. Dallas had tried a number of times to give Fish a companion, but none of the other goldfish had lasted more than a week. She would find the intended confidante floating lifelessly in the bowl after a day or two, with Fish going about his business quite oblivious to death being so close at hand.

Some things, she thought vaguely as she opened the container of fish food, were meant to go through life alone. Like her.

The goldfish seemed to swish a little harder at the sight of Dallas. When pressed, Dallas would have sworn that Fish responded like a true pet. But only when pressed.

"People will think I'm crazy if I talk about an affectionate goldfish," she murmured out loud, dropping in a few flakes of food. Fish came to life, darting toward the dark spots on his watery ceiling.

Dallas reached for the battered saucepan that stood empty on the back burner. She filled it half full of water, set it back on the burner and turned the gas on.

Tea, Dallas told herself. Tea was in order. She was too tired to whip up chicken soup, even though she felt she needed it. Given to living on hot dogs and beer at the stadium, she still shunned canned soups and their high salt content. A contradiction in terms, she knew, but that was her, a constant contraction in terms. She smiled to herself. Her father had called her that, along with a lot of other things.

She missed the tall, hulking man who had been her whole world up until three years ago.

"Don't start," she warned herself. "Not tonight." She would cry if she started thinking about him. She felt exceedingly lonely for some reason. She knew she had only to pick up the phone to contact any one of a number of people who would be willing to come over and help her spend her evening, but she was lonely in a darker, deeper sense. Vaguely she felt it had something to do with talking to Ryan today. Maybe that was why she resented him.

Resented? No, that was the wrong word.

"Well, what is the right word?" she asked Fish. There was no answer.

Rather than continue soul-searching, she turned her attention to her oncoming cold. She went to the pantry to look for a teabag. She knew there was a box somewhere in that jumbled mess. She had ferreted it out the last time she had come down with a cold, nine months ago.

"How long do tea bags last, Fish?" she asked. "No, I guess you wouldn't know, would you? Not something you indulge in. Don't start," she advised. "It's horrid. Tea's only good when you're sick." She pressed her hand to her forehead. Warm. A summer cold. How ridiculous. Oh well, getting annoyed wasn't going to help her.

"Neither is the tea if I can't find it," she muttered, pushing aside the unopened containers of spices she had bought in fits of domestic creativity that never lasted longer than the trip back from the grocery store.

The phone rang just as she spotted her quarry.

She grabbed the receiver from the wall cradle, reaching for the box of teabags with her other hand. "Yes?"

"Boy, you're in some mood tonight."

She cradled the yellow phone between her ear and shoulder and leaned against the wall. "Oh, hi, Rusty."

"Hi yourself. How come you were so hard on The Fox today?"

She smiled. "Someone has to be. Otherwise he's going to try walking on water any day now."

"You've got him all wrong."

She thought of the three curvaceous women at the bar and the smile on Ryan's lips as he began his autographing session. "Do I?"

"I'm just calling to make sure you've got all the facts right."

"I do. Don't worry. His professional record is safe with me." She laughed. "I didn't tarnish the fact that he's a game away from breaking Grover Cleveland Alexander's 1912 record for sixteen shutout games—"

"Or the fact that he's the only pitcher who's finished every game he's started," Rusty reminded her.

"The season's not over yet, my friend."

"You sound as if you're rooting for him to mess up."

A memory of Ryan's knowing look came back to her. "A little humility might do him good."

"What he's got he's earned."

"Hired you on as his PR man, has he?"

"I *like* the guy, Dallas."

"Everyone's entitled to a mistake in judgement once in a while," she quipped.

"And I think you're making it. He's really a nice guy."

"I haven't seen that side of him yet," she said carelessly. She pulled a chipped mug from her cupboard. "Did you call to defend him?"

"No, I called to tell you something."

She waited, but Rusty was obviously going to make her ask. "What?"

"He's coming over."

Dallas almost dropped the mug. "What!"

"You already said that."

"You gave him my address!" she accused.

"Roommates share things," he told her. "Bye."

"Rusty, how *could* you?" she cried, but the line was already dead.

The doorbell wasn't. It pealed loudly. Damn! Was that him? A hissing noise and the smell of smoke caught her attention. The pot! She had let the water boil away. Angrily she snatched the pan off the stove and marched toward the door.

She threw it open. "Yes?" she demanded.

Ryan was about to say a casual hello, but the word never came out. However he had expected her to look at home, it wasn't like this. She made quite a picture with her hair loose and slightly disarrayed about her shoulders, her long legs peering out from beneath the oversized shirt, and barefoot. He thought of Rusty's comment about his own requirements in women and smiled. It was only after a moment that he noticed the blackened interior of the pot she was holding.

"Been cooking?" he asked mildly. "Or do you intend to use that on me?"

He figured Rusty had called to warn her. But if he had, why was she standing in the doorway dressed like that? And what was she wearing under that shirt? He felt a tightness in the pit of his stomach. What was he doing here? he asked himself. He had enough on his mind without traipsing around Beverly Hills chasing after some woman with a chip on her shoulder, no matter how attractive she was.

He wasn't given to acting impulsively. Control was what had governed his life ever since he could remember. It was evident in the way he pitched, the way he batted, everything. He had mapped out his life at an early age, deciding exactly what he wanted and then going after it. First had come school and an education that would keep him permanently out of poverty. Baseball had followed. He had started late. Most players were tapped fresh out of high school or in their first year of college; he had come to the game at the age of twenty-two, with a degree in engineering in his pocket. He believed in leaving nothing to chance.

Yet here he was, taking a chance on having this woman slam the door in his face. Why? What was there about her that fascinated him so? She wasn't extraordinarily beautiful. No, not beautiful at all in the model sense. Rather than beauty there was something...striking about her. That was the word. Striking. And once struck, it stuck. He grinned at the weak rhyme.

"For a man who thinks he's going to get clobbered with a pan, you certainly are lighthearted." She made no move to step back. Instead she blocked the entrance with her arm high on the door jamb. The fact that it raised the hem of the shirt high on her thigh did not go unnoticed by Ryan. "Just why *are* you here?" she asked.

Damned if I know, he thought. I just wanted to see your face again, I guess, to convince myself that this charge I feel wasn't something I imagined. "I want to arrange another meeting with you."

"Oh?" Was this his strange way of asking for a date? she wondered. If it was, she was going to take great pleasure in turning him down.

"Yes, I didn't think the interview went off all that well. I thought maybe you could come by after tomorrow's game and we'll do it right."

Ryan smiled, almost magically negating her defensive feelings about his showing up on her doorstep. It was the Ryan Fox smile, Dallas thought. Electric.

Three hundred watts. Guaranteed to melt female fans in the stands at fifty paces. It wasn't doing such a poor job on her, either.

"Is that all?" she asked.

"No."

She waited. Nothing.

He was fumbling, damn it. He had never fumbled before. Never. Was it because she was Carlyle's daughter that he was having so much trouble? Or what? "Or what" loomed very large on the horizon.

"Well?" she asked finally. Her arm was getting tired. She slid it down the length of the jamb until it rested at her side.

What would that hand feel like running along the length of his body? he wondered. He was going to find out, he thought with determination. Before the season was over, he was going to find out.

"I want to see you again—privately."

"Again?" she echoed, not sounding nearly as haughty or aloof as she had planned. "I hardly think that twenty-five minutes at The Well constitutes seeing me in the sense you're implying." An odd sort of pleasure was slowly sweeping through her. A pleasure derived not from the idea of turning him down, but from . . . accepting him?

"Okay, I'd like to see you for the first time."

"I don't date ballplayers."

"Usually?"

"As a rule." He was crowding her without taking a single step forward. His presence was once again swamping her senses.

"Rules are made to be broken."

"Not my rules."

"Anyone's rules," he corrected her. "There are always exceptions."

"And you think you're one?"

He bent his face close enough to hers to kiss her. She felt his breath on her lips. "Yes." There was no egotism in his tone. "You'll see me, Dallas, without a pad in your hand." It was spoken as a simple fact.

For a moment she was sure he was going to kiss her, and despite everything she felt about the cavalier pitcher, she *wanted* him to.

But then, stunned, she watched him turn away. As she looked, her mouth dry, her senses reeling, her lips yearning for the feel of his, he walked away.

Just who the hell did he think he was?

Ryan heard the sound of the slamming door just before he turned the key in the ignition. A smile curved his lips as he nodded. Before the season was out, he promised himself.

Four

It never failed. The simple act of just walking into a baseball stadium made her tingle with excitement and anticipation. There was something in the air, a tension, an expectation of seeing new heroes created and old heroes living up to their reputations, that crackled all around her. Although she felt that baseball had undergone a change for the worse, she never lost the feeling. As far as she was concerned a baseball game was still a wonderful thing to witness, pompous ballplayers notwithstanding.

It brought back memories for her, memories she loved to relive. Baseball was more than just a game to Dallas; it represented a time in her life when she was happy, a time that she didn't want to let go. That was why she disliked the change in attitude among the players; it represented a break with the past.

Maybe, she speculated, that was why she had felt so hostile toward Ryan during the interview. He was the embodiment of the changes baseball had gone through. He was the new breed of player.

She liked the old breed better. Dallas could remember sitting in the first row, right behind third base, game after game, watching her father defend the tiny square like a wartime soldier defending his post. There would never be another player like him. Not for her.

Before she walked into the press box she approached a hot dog vendor who was working the pre-game crowd. She ordered two hot dogs with everything. It was a ritual. It helped to establish the proper atmosphere for her, helped her relive the past and enjoy the present.

"Hey, Dallas, what's cooking?"

Dallas walked into the tiny press box, a glass-enclosed cluster of seats situated just above home plate.

It was still early. There were only two other people in the box right now. The man who had hailed her sat relaxed in his chair wearing the T-shirt and faded jeans that were his trademark.

"Nothing much, Mike," Dallas answered as she took the seat adjacent to the paunchy man.

She could see Ryan out on the field throwing practice pitches. The catcher, a ruddy-faced man who reminded Dallas of Yogi Berra, was out on the field with him. They looked so intense that if she hadn't known better Dallas would have said the championship was riding on this game. Then she remembered that Ryan was out to break a record for shutouts. That explained his concentration.

"Heard you walked out on The Fox last night."

Dallas turned her attention from the players on the field to the man seated at her left. Taylor, the other man in the box, had stopped reviewing his notes and was also looking at her curiously.

"I didn't walk out on him. I was laying groundwork for my interview and three very eager fans pushed me out of the way. I decided that maybe that wasn't the best time or place for an in-depth interview."

Mike Wynter grinned. It was the kind of grin that told her he wasn't quite buying her story. "I hear he does his best interviews in small, dark places."

The man's eyes teased her. Dallas took a breath. Since she had become a sports reporter Wynter had always treated Dallas as if he expected her to faint or do something else that would satisfy his secret belief that the only sport a woman should cover was a needlepoint race. He also thought that every woman's heart palpitated madly at the sight of a good-looking male.

"I'm afraid he's going to have to do this one in a large, bright place." Her smile matched Mike's.

Mike shook his head. "They'll never believe this one at *The Sun*."

"Mike?" Dallas began as she unwrapped her first hot dog.

"Yeah?"

"I don't really care," she said sweetly.

Mike looked dubiously at Taylor, who shrugged and went back to his notes.

The noise level in the box grew as reporters began filing in. Ed Ashley, a tall, dark-skinned man on the San Diego newspaper, slid into the vacant seat next to Dallas. He held a crisp twenty over his head and looked around. "I've got twenty that says Fox blows this one."

Everyone knew Ashley was referring to the record Ryan was trying to break. He had already tied the record for shutouts, with sixteen to his credit for the year. But the season was almost over, and bets were running hot and heavy as to whether or not he would succeed in breaking a record that had stood since 1912.

Taylor rose quickly. "I'll take that bet."

"How about you, Dallas? You with me or are you bent on losing?" Ashley asked.

"Dallas likes being with a winner—at least part of the time," Mike chimed in, his cherubic face the picture of innocence.

Dallas looked out on the field. Ryan was standing there as if frozen in place. She could almost see him concentrating on the next pitch. His expression was somber, and he was looking at something that none of them could see. Then he swung his arm back and a perfectly controlled ball whistled into the catcher's glove.

"Count me in." Her eyes never left Ryan as she dug into her purse. "Twenty to break the record."

"You know something I don't?" Ashley asked good-naturedly as he took her money.

"She should. She was out with The Fox last night," Mike said lowering his voice conspiratorially as he leaned over her to get closer to Ashley.

Dallas pushed both men apart. "It was for an interview and it was at The Well. I was with the man for a whole twenty-five frustrating minutes. I didn't get more out of him than I could have gotten from a bio sheet."

"Try harder," Ashley urged.

"She intends to." Mike chuckled.

"I always complete an interview. My readers expect my best and that's what they get." She stared straight ahead. "My editor wants this piece as a feature in the Sunday magazine."

Ashley let out a whistle. "The Fox has come up in the world a little."

"Next he'll be hawking clothes in some commercial," Mike speculated.

"Or making it big in the movies," Ashley said, chuckling.

Dallas sat back, thoughtfully munching on her hot dog and watching Ryan. She wondered if what the men were saying would ultimately turn out to be true. Would he cash in on his popularity and make hay while the sun shone? Somehow she couldn't see him doing that. There was something about him that told her he'd stick with baseball as long as it would stick with him.

And, she reminded herself, at his salary he didn't need ads and movie roles to see him through.

She was surprised to see Ryan suddenly break his concentration. She saw him wave up to the stands, and then realized that it wasn't a fan he was waving to. It was her. Just for a moment her breath caught in her throat.

"Hey, he's got an eye for you, Dallas," Ashley said with a laugh.

"He'd wave at any woman who breathes." Dallas dismissed the incident, trying not to show that she was pleased by his attention.

Another reporter walked by and leaned over her chair from behind. He moved his head in close. "Be good to him, Carlyle. I've got a roll riding on them making it to the pennant."

That did it. Dallas stood up, nearly bumping heads with the man. "Everybody," she said in a loud clear voice, "I have an announcement to make."

The growing din subsided momentarily. "I am not, I repeat, *not* seeing Ryan T. Fox in any capacity other than as a reporter doing an interview. Is that understood?"

"Sure, Dallas, sure."

"Whatever you say, Dallas."

"Uh-huh."

"Got another fairy tale?"

From their responses she could tell that they all believed exactly the opposite. Dallas gave up and sat down. Let them think what they chose. She knew differently. She was going to see Ryan after the game and get some facts pinned down. After that she was only going to see him at each game until the season was over. Strictly business.

It wasn't strictly business, though, that made her unconsciously hold her breath each time Ryan was up on the mound once the game began. Each time a batter took a swing she curled her fingers into fists, waiting for the crack of the bat that would keep today's game from going down in the annals of baseball history. The knowing look she got from the other reporters each time the visitors' side was retired told her that she was the focus of almost as much attention as Ryan.

"Just worried about my bet," she told Ashley.

"I never thought anything else." He grinned broadly.

This is going to have to stop, Dallas told herself sternly, before it goes any further.

It was hot on the mound and getting hotter. Ryan felt perspiration running down his spine. Beneath the dark-blue cap with its blazing *R* his blond hair was soaked with sweat. His arm had long since begun aching, but there was another inning to go after this one. Gibson had already approached him twice about putting in a relief pitcher. It wasn't that the game was going badly. The score was 1-0 in their favor. But the manager was afraid that the combination of heat and tension might prove to be too much for his best pitcher.

It was 105 in the shade, and there wasn't any shade. The old joke echoed in Ryan's mind as he waited for the next batter. The second out had been called. One more, just one more to go, he thought, and then he could get back to the dugout. The idea of shade and a seat sounded pretty good from where he stood.

The idea of her body next to his sounded even better.

He reproached himself. He couldn't afford to let his thoughts drift. He needed his total concentration for this one. The Lions were sending out their best hitter, a tall, powerful slugger named Dan Wilson who wasn't very happy that he was 0 for 2 today.

Ryan wiped the sweat from his brow with the back of his right hand, the ball held firmly in his left. He was a southpaw, like Sandy Koufax, and extremely proud of it. The stray thought made him smile.

In response Wilson glared and took a few practice swings with his bat. Ryan glanced up past the first row of spectators behind home plate, past the lodge section, up to the press box. He could see her. Worse than that, he could smell her scent, or thought he could.

He muttered a curse under his breath. Top of the eighth, a powerhouse at the plate just itching to smash a home run, and he was thinking of the perfume she had worn last night.

The batter was ready.

Ryan forced thoughts of Dallas out of his mind as he wound up slow and easy. The call came. Outside. Ball one.

Damn, he had wanted that one straight in the pocket for a strike. Once again he cursed himself for letting his concentration slip and Dallas for making it go. He had never let a woman affect his game before. Hell, they had never even stayed in his mind for more than a few minutes at a time. There had never been any reason to think of them the way he was now thinking of Dallas.

It occurred to him that he had never wanted a woman before, the way he wanted her. Usually when desire nudged him the woman was already there, and more than willing. This one, though, was a challenge. This one was stubborn, independent, with a good head on her shoulders. He had a feeling that she was definitely going to be worth all the effort he could put forth.

He caught sight of Gibson out of the corner of his eye. The heavyset manager was pacing back and forth by the dugout, his eyes never leaving the pitcher's mound.

Ryan looked back at home plate. The batter held the bat as if he were willing it to make contact for him. Ryan threw the ball.

"By the numbers. Strike one."

The umpire's call made him smile. The pitch had gone just as he had planned it. He allowed himself another quick look toward Dallas.

Dallas could have sworn they made eye contact just then. With the stadium crammed full of Rebels fans— of Fox fans, most likely—she couldn't escape the feeling that he had looked directly up at her.

"Hey, Dallas, you blushing?" Ashley asked.

"No," she said easily, covering her queasy feeling with a grace she had learned long ago. "That's flushing, not blushing. It's hot in here." The air-conditioning had decided to take a powder in face of the heat, and they were all perspiring heavily, waiting for the game to end so they could retreat to their typewriters.

Dallas was trying to compose her column as she watched, hoping to get most of it down in her mind before she had to go down to meet Ryan.

Had to. The words rolled around in her head. She felt as if she didn't have a choice. She knew that even without the interview as an excuse she would see him just the way he had asked. Maybe not today, but tomorrow, or the day after. Perhaps not here, perhaps on the road, but somewhere, sometime, somehow, she knew she was going to be with him. It seemed inevitable.

The thought scared her.

She didn't like the inevitable, didn't like not having a say in things. They hadn't kissed, yet she felt a pull toward him.

Would she have no peace until she found out what it would be like to be kissed by him? And would that give her peace, she wondered cryptically, or open up a whole new field of battle?

"Strike three!" Mike called out cheerfully, eyeing Ashley. "Get that twenty ready, Ashley. It's going to have a new home."

"The game is not over yet, Wynter."

No, Dallas thought, the game isn't over yet. She pressed her lips together and vowed to fight whatever it was that Ryan was doing to her. She didn't want a quick affair with a baseball great-of-the-moment. She had seen his type time and again before. Riding the crest of the crowd's adulation, they were all young, all handsome, and all completely thoughtless when it came to women. Clamoring fans offering what passed for love, and the pressure of the game didn't give them any time to think. She wanted no part of that.

But did she have a choice?

"Hell, he can do everything with that ball but make it sit up and beg," Mike commented in admiration, then wrote the sentence down.

"That," Dallas said crisply, "he probably saves for his dates."

Ryan undoubtedly wanted to make sure she wrote a favorable article, she told herself, waiting for the Rebels' first batter to come out on the field. That was why he had come on to her.

She sat up, alert. The batter walking onto the field was Ryan. By definition pitchers were notoriously poor hitters. Ryan was the exception that broke the rule. He could hit as well as any of them. He was no Hank Aaron, but he could certainly hold his own, she thought, realizing that she was defending him again.

You're going soft on the man, she told herself. Let him make good on his promise of a date and you'll be running him for president. She sat up straighter, annoyed with her thoughts.

"That interested, eh?" Ashley prodded. She didn't have to look to know he was grinning.

"I'm waiting for him to strike out," Dallas said matter-of-factly. "I want to get out of this sweatbox before I dissolve into a puddle." She pushed her plastered bangs from her forehead for emphasis.

"Uh-huh," Ashley answered in a singsong manner.

Dallas frowned and said nothing, even after Ryan got a base hit.

She chewed her lower lip for the remainder of the game. The Lions' relief pitcher retired the Rebels after the fifth batter up hit a foul ball to deep left field. Ryan was back on the mound again.

Later she couldn't remember breathing while the next three batters were at the plate. The next thing she knew was that Mike was clapping her on the back and crowing for Ashley to pay up. She felt Ashley stick something in her hand and looked down. It was a twenty.

"Well, at least I got the heading for my column today," Ashley said good-naturedly. "'Fox smashed 1912 record.'"

The crowd was still going wild as the Rebels surged out onto the field and surrounded Ryan. The manager was giving him a ferocious bear hug.

"You'd think they'd won the pennant," Dallas muttered under her breath, trying to deny the thrill she was feeling herself.

"They will," Mike said to her.

"I'll put twenty on that!" another reporter called from the rear of the room. Mike turned to accept the bet.

Dallas eased herself out of the press box. The air was heavy, and the shouts of exuberant fans filled her ears. It was going to be impossible to see him, she decided, with all this adulation going on. He was going to be totally caught up in the partying. She could continue the interview tomorrow, she told herself. She still had time.

Everywhere she looked the crowd was alive with enthusiasm. Not only had their team won, but they had been there to see history made. History, she thought dryly as she tried to make her way along, that would be unmade at some time in the future. But for now Ryan was their hero.

"Sorry, Grover, ol' boy," she said to the memory of the last record holder. "You can't win 'em all."

"Hey, Dallas!"

She turned at the sound of her name. She looked around for the source, then shrugged. She must have imagined it.

"Dallas!"

This time it was a bellow, and this time she saw who it was. Rusty was in the stands fifty feet away from her. The fifty feet were filled with fans, asking for autographs.

"What are you doing here?" Dallas had to practically burrow her way to him.

"Wait your turn, lady!" a man said gruffly, elbowing her back.

"I've already had my turn, thanks," she said lightly. The man eyed her doubtfully.

"Foxy said to be sure to come down and meet him," Rusty called over the head of a red-headed woman who produced three balls for him to sign.

"I thought with all the commotion..." Dallas began, looking for a way out.

Rusty nodded. "That's what he said you'd say."

Oh, so now he thought he could read her mind, did he? she thought, annoyed at being so predictable.

"He said to tell you that he'd like you to come down to the locker room."

"Why? So he can growl about my being there again?"

Rusty gave the last ball back to the redhead, extended his arm toward Dallas and all but dragged her to him.

"'Scuse me, folks, that's all for now. Let me get out of these wet clothes and I'll sign all the autographs you want," he promised with a wide grin. "Right now The Fox wants to see his lady."

Everyone looked after Dallas with envy as she followed Rusty, fuming.

Five

$\overline{\hspace{3cm}}$

I am *not* his lady," Dallas protested as Rusty led her away. "How could you say something like that?"

Rusty smiled at her over his shoulder, shrugging at the same time. "Hell, it'll give them something to talk about. What do you really have against him, anyway?"

They reached the locker room, and he pushed opened the door for her. Dallas blinked as her eyes became accustomed to the dimly lit corridor. "He's too damn sure of himself, for one thing."

Rusty gave her a sidelong glance. "There's a lot of that going around."

He'd always known how to take a swipe at her and get away with it. "All right, I'll ease up." She looked down at his hand. "You can let go of me now. I promise not to run away."

He released her hand. "Damn, there goes my excuse for hanging on to a beautiful woman."

She laughed. "Rusty, you're incorrigible."

"If you say so," he all but shouted. The noise level had become almost deafening as they approached the locker room.

Reporters, newscasters and minicams were all tangled together like dancers performing a grotesque ritual. She sidestepped a Channel 8 reporter who was determined to get Ryan on camera. In the center of the noisy circle Ryan was looking, she thought, weary behind the wide smile he was offering the reporters. He was trying his level best to be civil, but she had learned enough about him to know that he would have loved to shove them all aside and get to his well-deserved shower.

"How did it feel, Fox?" someone shouted.

"It felt great!" he responded.

"And now?"

"Still great."

The mindless questions must annoy him, Dallas thought, a smile curving her lips.

Rusty noted her expression and grinned to himself. His hunch had been right. Dallas was sparring with Fox because she was attracted to him. There was no other explanation for her strange behavior toward the man, not if he examined the situation closely. She was too levelheaded, too straightforward, for him to accept this sudden change in behavior without questioning it. He would be willing to bet anything that Champ's little girl was falling in love. She just didn't know it yet. Wait until he called Laurie.

"Look, why don't you boys just give the man a chance to wash some of the sweat away?" Gibson urged, using his bulk to block the cameramen. "Hey, Delaney, c'mere," Gibson called to the first-baseman, beckoning him onward with a rapid motion of his hand.

Delaney, a man who looked as if he would be more at home in a football jersey than a baseball uniform, lumbered over on cue.

"Why don't you tell all these newscasters about that triple play you pulled off in the fourth inning while Fox here takes his shower, okay?" He pushed Ryan toward the stalls, following him like a tail gunner.

"This is our chance," Rusty said, pulling Dallas after him.

"The man wants a shower," Dallas pointed out, but she permitted herself to be shoved through the inner doors.

"The man wants to see you even more than he wants a shower."

"Why?" Dallas's suspicions were aroused.

Rusty just grinned. "Why don't you ask him yourself?"

Gibson turned around at the sound of their voices. "Dallas?" He was surprised to see her on the inner side of the locker room doors.

Dallas held her hands up before he could comment on her being there. "I was forced in. I'm innocent."

Ryan passed her on the way to the shower area and gave her a wink that said her innocence would be something he would look forward to exploring later on.

She really should put him in his place, she told herself as she stared after him. Right then and there, with a few well-chosen words. She was no newcomer to the neat putdown. But for some reason no words came. That annoyed her even more.

The reporters suddenly rolled in like a tidal wave, wires, voices and cameras all coming at once. The walls seemed to strain as they flooded the room. Gibson, a short man despite his girth, stood up on the nearest bench to make himself heard. "All right, so you didn't like Delaney's story. I promise, let Fox shower and get dressed and he'll give you something you can sink your teeth into. But he's not very accommodating when he's dirty."

Muttering met his statement.

Dallas saw Rusty motioning to her. "Now what?" she asked.

"This way," he mouthed.

Curious, she followed him, taking care to do so unobtrusively. She could have spared herself the bother. The reporters' attention was trained on the entrance to the showers.

"I'm beginning to feel a little ridiculous. This isn't going to wind up being another of your practical jokes, is it?" she asked suspiciously.

"Are you kidding?" Rusty asked, leading her through a back exit to the parking lot, rolling his eyes in mock innocence. "Foxy'd have my head."

"Since when are you afraid of any teammate?" she scoffed.

"Since we started sharing the same room. When he's not pitching he pumps iron. One wrong move and I'll wake up with a two hundred pound barbell across my chest."

She thought about commenting on that, but let it drop. "Just where are we going?"

"Back through the parking lot. He'll meet us," Rusty whispered. They were alone, but he wasn't taking any chances.

"Then why—" Dallas realized that she was whispering, too, and it struck her as ridiculous. She raised her voice to its normal level. "Then why did you take me to the locker room?" None of this was making any sense to her, not the exaggerated charade, nor her own reactions to it. The idea of meeting Ryan on the sly actually appealed to her—even if it was just to complete an interview. She might as well admit it, she thought. She had fallen victim to the Fox charm, and he hadn't done so much as proposition her. That, she was sure, was coming. Well, she would deal with it when the time came.

"To let him see you."

"Why?" she pressed, bewildered.

"So he'd know I got to you before you had a chance to leave."

"Why?" she repeated again.

She was hard-nosed, just like her dad, he thought affectionately. "Let's just say that what he has in mind by way of celebration doesn't include a lot of cameramen and reporters." He relished the effect his words were having on Dallas. If any other ballplayer had shown signs of this much interest in Dallas, he would have gone out of his way to derail the man's plans. But Ryan was different. Beneath the reputation, beneath the slow, easy smile, was a man another man could really like. More than that, Fox was a man another man could really trust.

Rusty let her over to a blue Corvette, then stopped.

Dallas glanced at the car, then shifted her gaze to Rusty. "Just what *does* he have in mind by way of celebration?"

"Why don't you ask him?" Rusty prompted, nodding behind her.

Dallas turned and saw Ryan coming toward them, his gait hurried. There was an unconscious sensuality in every move he made. He was all man, all right. Lucky thing for her, Dallas thought, that she was too aware of his appeal to get caught by it.

His hair was damp from a quick shower, and his clothes looked hastily thrown on. He carried his Stetson in his hand. Haste looked good on him, she thought.

"Enjoy your evening." Rusty melted away into the slowly encroaching twilight.

The evening was sultry, and the warm air carried her scent to Ryan for real this time. He hadn't been sure she would come, even with Rusty's prodding. He had hurried, not worried about the reporters who stood like hungry vultures at the mouth of the locker room, but afraid that if he took too long she would change her mind and go.

"You came."

"I had precious little choice in the matter," she said lightly, covering her growing case of nerves. "Rusty all but threw me over his shoulder and carried me here fireman style."

"He's a great roommate." Ryan grinned, gesturing toward the car.

She hesitated for a moment, then decided to go along. She could always stop the merry-go-round if she wanted to, right? She tucked her skirt in beneath her as she sat down. "Where are we going?" she asked.

"Just away." He gunned the engine. "We have an interview to finish, remember?"

"I do, but I wasn't sure if you did. Some pretty heady stuff's happened to you since we last met."

The grin was charming. It made him look partly like a bashful, disbelieving farm boy and partly like a self-satisfied star. "I guess you might say that."

Dallas watched the scenery whiz by them as they peeled out of the lot and onto the road. "Um, Fox?"

"Yes?"

"You really don't have to drive the way you pitch, you know."

He looked down at his speedometer and saw the needle trembling between seventy and seventy-five. "Sorry, I guess my adrenaline hasn't stopped going yet."

"That's not the only thing that's going." She nodded behind them.

Ryan looked into his rearview mirror and saw a motorcycle cop, his lights flashing brightly against the darkened sky, quickly closing the distance between them.

"Guess dinner will have to wait," Ryan muttered, pulling onto the shoulder and fishing his wallet out of his jeans.

This was the first time he had mentioned dinner, and Dallas was about to protest that all she wanted was an interview when the policeman appeared at Ryan's window.

The policeman scowled darkly as he leaned down to the window. "Fire, buddy?" he asked.

"Sorry, Officer, I didn't have my mind on my driving," Ryan apologized.

Well, at least he wasn't trying to impress the policeman with who he was, Dallas thought, unconsciously giving Ryan another point in his favor.

The policeman looked down at the license Ryan offered, and Dallas saw the man's mouth comically drop open. He looked from the picture to Ryan. "You're

Ryan Fox," the officer said, suddenly turning from a threat into a fan right before Dallas's eyes. She closed them, sensing what was coming next.

Five minutes later Ryan left with a warning as the patrolman drove off with an autograph tucked inside his shirt pocket.

"Certainly seems to be your lucky night," Dallas commented. She leaned her head against the back of the seat.

"So far." He looked at her. The smile he gave her was soft and hit the core of her stomach without warning.

Keep this up and you'll be heading his fan club before the night's out, she warned herself.

He took her to a small, intimate restaurant that was, she would have thought, totally against type. Except that by now she was beginning to admit that she really had no idea exactly what "type" Ryan T. Fox was. And more than that, she admitted to herself that perhaps she had been overreacting to his image because she had been afraid of what might happen between them from the very start. Caring for him might dismantle her entire world.

"You're not anything like the stories about you," she allowed herself to say as she toyed with the rich chocolate mousse she knew she shouldn't have ordered. The owner of the restaurant, a large, smiling man who looked at Ryan with parental pride showing in his face, had urged it on her, and she had no willpower when it came to anything chocolate, a fact that Ryan seemed to have discovered with glee.

"That's what I've been trying to tell you."

"Appearances aren't everything," she murmured as she made short work of the last of her dessert. She was going to hate herself the next time she stepped on a scale, she thought.

"Okay," she said when their after-dinner drinks were placed before them. "So I have your background straight. And your motivation," she added as an afterthought.

"That," he said, rolling the word carefully over his tongue, "I'm not sure about."

The look he gave her was so intense that she felt as if he could see right through her, as if he were looking into her soul, seeing all her secrets. She wasn't ready for that, even though she was beginning to mellow toward him.

All through the meal, with the courses and the questions coming as if there were no end, she had felt things happening to her. While she kept up a zesty banter, living up to the image of C. C. Carlyle's little girl, she had felt Ryan affecting her.

"So where does Ryan Fox go from here?" she asked in a voice that sounded strangely subdued.

Ryan moved closer along the corner banquette they were sharing until their thighs were touching. He put his arm around her, just touching her shoulders. She didn't move; she hardly breathed. He touched her cheek with his other hand, his fingers curved along the hollow in the same controlled way they did when he curled them around a baseball. Controlled, yet gentle.

"To a few more winning seasons, I hope," he told her softly.

It was hard for both of them to keep their minds on the actual conversation. Her throat felt dry. She reached for her drink, never looking away from him. "And then?"

"And then," he said with a smile, his fingers making love to her cheek, "I'd like to finally talk my dad into letting me update the farm and do with it what should be done."

It was a strange sentiment for a man with an engineering degree, she thought. But she liked the sound of it. Filial affection was something she could relate to. "You mean your father still lives on the same farm you grew up on?"

The dim lighting caressed his hair, catching the highlights. Dallas curled her hand in her lap to keep from tracing the outline of his face.

"Yep. Stubborn man, my dad. Won't take a helping hand from any of us, even though he was always there when we needed him."

Dallas smiled fondly, his words taking her to another time, another place. "That sounds like my father." She sipped a little of her drink. The brandy found its way into her veins, warming her. The evening, the man and the drink made her feel strangely vulnerable. He was affecting her again, just like the first time, at The Well. He made her feel the need to be taken care of, and she didn't want to feel that way. She had been independent since her father had died, shutting out the pain that attachment brought with it.

He saw the light of discomfort flicker through her eyes and wondered if it had been caused by something he'd said. He searched for a safe topic. "I used to read your dad's column every morning before I started my chores."

It gave them another link, and she smiled, still silent.

How would she take to being comforted? he wondered. "I was really upset when I read about his heart attack."

She could tell by his voice that he was being genuine. This wasn't one of the platitudes she had received from strangers who didn't know her, hadn't known him, but felt obligated to say something when they found out whose daughter she was.

Dallas fought to keep herself from sinking into the sadness that went with the memory of the end. "The heart attack was the best thing that could have happened to him at the time," she said crisply. She saw a shocked look pass over Ryan's face. Did he think she was cold? she wondered. "The stroke he had the year before put him out of commission, brought him to his knees the way nothing else could have."

She looked away, twirling the stem of her glass slowly. "He *hated* being incapacitated, and I hated seeing him that way." She remembered how helpless he had looked, lying there against the white sheets, how drained, how lost. She shuddered.

Ryan reached out and put his hand over hers. She hardly seemed to notice.

"That big, vital man was reduced to being a lump in a bed, watching baseball games on TV and getting

flowers he didn't notice, telegrams he didn't read."
She choked on her words and was quiet.

He allowed her her moment of silence. Instinctively he knew that she would respond better to unspoken feelings. He pressed her hand gently, letting her know he cared.

Dallas looked up, her green eyes shining with tears. "I'm sorry. I don't usually talk about him this way."

"I'm glad you did."

She hunted through her purse for a tissue. He offered her a handkerchief before she found one. "Why?" she asked, taking it. She dabbed at her eyes.

"It lets me share a part of you that's hidden."

She looked at him, weighing his words. He could see her nervousness emerging. "Let's get on with the interview, okay?" She handed the handkerchief back to him, and he saw the curtain go down over her emotions.

They walked out to the parking lot half an hour later. A flash of white caught her eye at the far end of the lot. A sea gull had snared a piece of bread that had been carelessly thrown away.

"He should be out catching fish."

"Maybe he likes junk food," Ryan quipped. He liked the way she looked in the moonlight. He wanted to make love to her in the moonlight on an isolated beach, where only the two of them existed and the only sound they heard would be the waves caressing the shore. "Do I make you nervous?" he asked softly.

He saw her expression tighten as she watched the sea gull fly off. "Yes."

"Why?"

"I don't know how to read you."

He stopped at his car and opened the door for her. "I'm a very uncomplicated man."

She sat down, but waited to speak until he got in himself. "Any man who has an agent, enough money in the bank to patch a hole in the national debt and scads of adoring fans is not uncomplicated."

"Okay." He laughed, starting the car. "I'm as uncomplicated as my situation will permit." He turned to her just before he guided the car out of the near-empty lot. "Right now, I'm thinking some very uncomplicated thoughts."

"Such as?" She felt excitement taking hold. Idiot, she told herself. He might just be talking about Saturday's game. Yet her excitement refused to dissipate.

"Such as what it will be like to kiss you when I bring you home."

"That's not uncomplicated," she said in a small voice.

"Oh?" He watched the way his headlights cut through the night. "And why is that so complicated?"

"I told you, I don't go out with baseball players. That includes kissing them." She stiffened in her seat, once again sensing that something inevitable was about to happen.

"And I said that rules were made to be broken." He stopped for a red light and flashed her a grin that did more to dispel the darkness than the headlights did, she thought. "Besides, you went out with me tonight."

"To finish my story."

"And to start something else."

"I . . ." She got no further as her voice trailed off.

"Tell me that you really don't want to see me."

"I really don't want to see you."

"I don't believe you."

"That's because I'm lying."

He laughed and turned his head quickly to kiss her as he waited for the light to turn green.

That was it, just a quick, sweet kiss, over before it started. She had thought that her first kiss from him would make a volley of cannons go off, not be delivered in an instant while waiting for the light to change.

And yet, fleeting though it had been, it made her hunger for fulfillment and for things to come.

"I left my car at the stadium," she reminded him, fighting the tingle that was going through her limbs.

He glanced at her as he took the long winding road to her house. "I'll have someone bring it to you in the morning if you give me the keys." He knew that she was making a last-ditch attempt to force them to go their separate ways. "I won't crowd you, Dallas," he promised. "I have time. Haven't you noticed? I'm a master at waiting."

She thought of the times he had stood on the mound, watching the batter, judging just how the man would react to the next pitch.

"This isn't a game," she told him.

"All of life is a game," he contradicted. "And I take my games very seriously." He stopped the car.

They were home. Her home. She started to get out and realized that her knees felt shaky. She was afraid, but of what? Of feeling, probably. She knew that falling for Ryan Fox would be the worst thing she could do. She hurried toward her door.

"I don't intend to race you to the door," he called, and she stopped, feeling slightly foolish. She turned and saw that his smile wasn't mocking. "And I won't wrestle with you in order to get inside."

His voice was soft, gentle, as if he were trying to calm the turmoil within her. "What are you afraid of, Dallas?" he asked as he walked up to her.

His hands rested gently on the swell of her hips. He guided her to him almost without her knowing it. She felt the heat of the evening, the heat of his body, merging into one.

"You," she said without embarrassment, her green eyes holding his. The word was a whisper.

"Why? I'm a very unthreatening man," he told her just before he covered her lips with his own.

Six

Sultry sensations soared through Dallas, combining with emotions she wasn't prepared to deal with, wasn't sure she *wanted* to deal with. But there was no time to prepare. Only to feel.

His fingers tightened about her waist, pressing her to him ever so slightly as his kiss deepened. His lips caressed her mouth, draining it of all protests, making her soft and supple. She wasn't independent anymore. She was very, very dependent on what was happening.

She had never known a kiss could be so overwhelming, nor that a mouth could taste so sweet.

Ryan's hands left her waist and gently massaged her spine, following the path that the lightning bolts had taken as they jolted through her.

He felt her resistance diminishing. If he forced the situation there was no telling where the evening would end. He knew that the same desire churning within him was shared by Dallas. The thought occurred to him that she might say no, and he realized that he would actually welcome that. It would make her different, and he needed someone different. If she gave in she would be like all the others. At the moment he was content to satisfy himself with hope rather than risk being disappointed by reality.

He was releasing her. The thought registered slowly. Dallas opened her eyes, dazed and disoriented. For a split second she had been transported, had forgotten everything except the magic flowing in her veins, the magic his mouth was creating for her. She was surprised that he hadn't tried to press his advantage. Surprised and grateful.

He saw a different light in her eyes, a look of appraisal. They would reach an understanding soon, he thought. It helped ease the ache he felt.

"I'd better be going," he said as he lingered at her doorway.

"Yes, you'd better." She made no move toward her door. "Fox?"

He could see her verve returning. It made him smile. "Yes?"

"Why didn't you try for more just then?"

Well, she was straightforward enough, he thought. But he wouldn't have expected less. C. C. Carlyle hadn't been known for mincing words. "I'm not sure, really. I'm groping my way through all this," he admitted. "I've certainly met more cooperative women."

She thought of the three in the bar. "I'm sure you have."

He ran his knuckles along her cheek, and Dallas struggled not to react. "But cooperation isn't my first priority," he said quietly.

"Nice to know." She tried to sound distant, removed, like a sports reporter taking notes, not like a woman whose pulse was racing. "What is?"

"A woman who's real, who sees beyond the glitter and the fame."

He was describing her, she thought. He was taking his best ball and pitching it to her. Was she going to catch it? she wondered. And for how long?

This time Dallas turned and opened the door, then moved to step inside. She turned back, her hand resting on the doorknob. "Good luck in your quest."

"I think I might be on the right trail."

"Maybe" was all she said as she began to close the door.

His hand went out quickly, stopping her. "Rusty's having a barbecue tomorrow down at Dana Point."

"Yes, I know."

"Can I take you?"

She hesitated. How ethical was it to be dating a man on a team she was being paid to cover? She knew she was hiding behind excuses, but for the moment excuses were all she had between her and an uncertain future.

He winked as he turned to leave. "I'll be here at ten."

"I haven't said yes," she called after his departing figure.

"We'll negotiate. That's something else I'm good at," he threw over his shoulder, along with a smile. It was the same smile that had been captured in so many instant replays, the same one he wore when he made good.

Dallas closed the door behind her and leaned against it, her eyes shut. She was having her own instant replay. His after-shave came back to her, along with the taste of his mouth, the feel of his hands along her body, and the awful, empty yearning that had filled her when he stopped.

Then she recalled another image, one faded by time, but just as vivid, just as real. She saw a little girl sitting on the floor beside a front door, listening to the sound of footsteps fading, listening to the sound of being left alone. It was something she carried with her. She had seen countless marriages break under the pressures of the game. Her parents' hadn't been the first, and it wouldn't be the last. Why in heaven's name was she setting herself up for a fall like that?

"I won't do it," she announced flatly, walking into the kitchen. "I just won't do it. He can take his smile and his kisses and find another 'real woman' somewhere."

She glanced at the fishbowl and realized that it was past Fish's dinnertime. Reaching into the cupboard directly over the bowl, she found the slender cylinder of food, then shook several flakes into the water. Fish immediately leaped for them.

"And well might you leap," she commented, thinking not of the goldfish but of the way her heart had leaped at Ryan's very first kiss. She was susceptible to him. She had two choices: run from the fact, or face it. She bit her lip thoughtfully. She could always skip the picnic, but she had already promised Laura. And besides, that would be running.

"And C. C. Carlyle's little girl doesn't run," she told Fish. "Just because I'm going to the picnic with him doesn't mean I have to spend time with him once I get there."

She kicked off her shoes and sat down at the small kitchen table. Pushing thoughts of Ryan from her mind, she rummaged around for a pencil and paper. She needed to frame her thoughts about the man before they fled. One more session with him ought to do it, she decided. She would have her feature-length article and, hopefully, Darcy's newly won acknowledgement that she could deliver something more than just a sports story.

She was approaching this interview from a human-interest angle, finding the man behind the ball, she thought with a smile. She hoped it would allow her to move on in the field. Baseball was changing, *had* changed a lot since she had followed her father from town to town. She had discovered that she couldn't get used to the changes. Maybe the best thing was to get

away from the game altogether. At least she wanted to
have that option. Writing this article and proving herself might just do it for her.

L.A. had two home teams, and up until last week
she had been covering the Trojans. But then Arnold
had left, leaving a hole, and she had volunteered to
switch. The Rebels had been her father's beat, and
now they looked as if they were going to win the divisional title. It was her last-ditch attempt to salvage her
attitude about things. If being with the Rebels didn't
bring back the old times, the old feelings, then nothing would.

There was a warm spot in her heart for the Rebels,
and they were having a winning season. Finally. No
other team had come so far so fast this year. They had
started out in last place and surprised everyone. But
then, they had gained Ryan, she thought ruefully.

The Trojans had been given to Kiley, who had been
doing general sports coverage. Someone new had been
chosen to cover that desk. A game of musical chairs,
Dallas thought. But she was twenty-seven now, she
reminded herself. It was time to stop moving and to
listen to the tune being played. Traveling around, following a team, had been fun, but now there was a different yearning setting in, a desire to do something
beyond team reporting, something with more scope,
more depth.

The yearning went beyond that, she knew. She
wanted a home and family. She wanted stability. For
three years she had denied that, clinging unrealisti-

cally to baseball in hopes of keeping her hold on the
past. But ever since her father had died she had felt
alone, rootless. Even though she had a house, even
though she belonged to the family of baseball players, it wasn't enough. She wanted, *needed*, to belong
to some*body*, somebody stable. She wasn't going to
find that somebody by spending eleven weeks straight
on the road, trailing after a team when they played out
of town.

Dallas frowned. She certainly wasn't going to find
what she needed by falling for baseball's current de-
ity, no matter what he said about wanting to find a real
woman. She went on making notes.

"Not bad, not bad at all."

Ryan was referring to her white shorts and hot-pink
halter with its white trim. He stood in her doorway,
casually dressed in gray jeans and a light-blue pull-
over, looking every bit the heartthrob. He had arrived early, but she was ready for him. Or as ready as
she could be.

She had planned on wearing a pair of white slacks
and a jersey, but the weather had had other ideas. The
temperature had soared up to a very unaccommodat-
ing ninety-seven degrees by nine. There was no need to
suffer just because she was afraid, she had told herself sternly. She could hold him off just as well in
shorts as she could in slacks. Besides, she didn't have
anything that he hadn't seen over and over again on
other women, and probably in more ample amounts.

Ryan's dark eyes skimmed over her figure, ending with her sable hair, which was piled high in a careless knot.

"Thank you," she said politely.

"You smell good, too," he said, drawing closer.

"That's insect repellent," she answered dryly. "Shall we go?"

He would rather have stayed and made love to her, forgetting all his well-laid plans. He had been up half the night lying awake and thinking of her, reliving their kiss over and over and anticipating the moment when he could hold her, warm and willing, in his arms.

He nodded. "Party's already started, and it's a long drive to Dana Point." He ushered her out to his car. The top was down, and he looked at her uncertainly.

She read his mind. "I like the top down."

"Another point in your favor," he told her, holding the door open for her.

Just how did she rate in his eyes? she wondered, then cursed herself for caring.

"How's the article coming?" he asked, getting in next to her.

"Well," she said, flashing him a secretive smile and giving him no more detail than that. He pulled out of her driveway with a jerk. Her hand shot out as she braced herself against the dashboard. "Fox, I suggest that this time we try driving, not flying. Not every policeman on the force is a Rebels fan."

Obligingly he slowed down. He grinned at her, a touch of sheepishness in his smile. "When I was a kid

I always dreamed about having a fast, sleek car that opened up full throttle when I put my hand to it.''

"And fast, sleek women who did the same?" she ventured.

Was she back to that again? he wondered impatiently. "I thought we'd gotten beyond that." He frowned.

"Just asking," she said simply. "It's the reporter in me."

He knew better. "It's the woman in you," he corrected. "And yes, that's what I thought I wanted until I got it. It wasn't the same as the car," he admitted. He glanced at her and watched the way the wind played with her hair, pulling tendrils loose. "Are you sure you don't want the top up and the air-conditioning on?"

"This is fine," she assured him. "I've got a comb. Don't worry."

"Worrying is the last thing I do."

"Even before a game?"

"Especially before a game," he said. "It ruins my concentration. Besides, worrying never accomplished anything."

And then, for no reason at all, he slipped his hand over hers as he drove.

There was that warm feeling again, she thought. "Don't you need two hands?"

"Can't," he said. "I need one hand to steer."

"That's as old as the hills," she pointed out. It was, but there was something adorably corny about it when he said the line. He wasn't all fox. There was a pussy-cat mixed in there somewhere, a warm, adorable kitten that brought out all sorts of fond feelings in her.

"So is what I'm feeling."

"Drive, Fox," she instructed, keeping her face straight, her eyes forward. But he noticed that she didn't withdraw her hand. "We'll be late."

"I thought you wanted me to slow down."

Fast or slow, she was beginning to realize that either way she was sunk.

The path toward the park was rustic and reminded Ryan of home. He'd been thinking a lot about home lately, about bringing Dallas there and showing her off. He wondered what she would say when he told her. They hadn't even had a second date. In fact he knew that if he asked her, she would say they hadn't even had a first one. Even so, he had made up his mind about her. That was part of what his control was all about, knowing his own mind. And he knew with every fiber of his being that he wanted her. He wasn't certain how it would all turn out, just as he hadn't been certain about baseball when he got into the minors, but he knew what he wanted. He wanted her.

"Hey, will you look at that?" Rusty nudged his wife as Ryan and Dallas walked toward them. "Look who arrived together."

Laura, a petite blonde whose hands were filled with a tray piled high with hamburgers, looked over to where her husband was pointing. A frown slid over her face. "I didn't think that Dallas went in for ballplayers like Fox."

"Honey, there *ain't* no ballplayer like Foxy," Rusty corrected her.

"That's what all my friends say," Laura answered with a smile.

"I'm talking about on the field," he told her, knowing full well just what Laura's friends would be likely to say about Ryan. "Hey, we'd just about given up on you two," he called.

Dallas slid her sunglasses down onto her nose with a decisive movement. "I had to hitch a ride. Someone hasn't seen about getting my car back to me from the stadium."

"Oops." Ryan flashed her a apologetic smile.

"Yes, oops. If you played as well as you kept promises the Rebels would be in the basement instead of where they are."

"She has a way with words," Ryan said to Rusty.

"So they tell me," his friend answered. "Are you two still at it?"

Dallas smiled serenely. "Why, Rusty, I haven't the slightest idea what you mean." She looked around and spotted someone she knew near one of the barbecue pits. "Hey, Collins!" she called out. "Ready for the Series?"

Ryan watched her go, the slight sway of her hips reminding him just how much control he really did have when he needed it.

But he didn't have time to contemplate her curves or his control for long. Within moments he was surrounded by a ring of children. "Hey, Ryan, what kept ya?" a tow-headed boy of about twelve asked.

"Scottie's as demanding as you are," Ryan said to Rusty, nodding his head at Rusty's youngest.

"He gets it from his mother, not me." Rusty held up his hands innocently. Laura bumped the tray into his stomach, and his hands went down in reaction as she presented him with it.

"Make yourself useful."

Rusty kissed the curve of her neck quickly. "I thought I already had, darling'."

Laura walked back to the van, laughing heartily.

"Certainly doesn't do much for my ego," Rusty commented with a sigh.

"You two gonna talk, or you gonna play?" Scottie demanded, looking from his father to Ryan.

"Play, partner," Ryan assured him, taking off his Stetson and tossing it casually on the grass. "Now where's the ball?"

No sooner had Ryan finished his question than Scottie had thrust a ball into his hand. Two children behind him began to push Ryan toward a large open field.

"See you later," Rusty called out gleefully. "I'll tell Dallas that you've been kidnapped by determined munchkins."

There was no need to tell Dallas. Although she was busy talking to Collins and another player, she kept

Ryan in her sights. There was still part of her that had expected him to avail himself of the company of several young women who had come to the party unattached. She was both amused and delighted that his attention was taken by a group of children. For the next half hour, as Dallas mingled and ate the food that Laura kept urging on her, she watched Ryan play ball with the kids, and it warmed her heart.

Finally the game was over. When she saw Ryan looking her way Dallas quickly turned, not wanting him to know that she had been staring at him almost the entire time. She was deeply into a heated discussion about batting averages when she felt a kiss on the back of her neck. A kiss that shot arrows through her. Startled, she swung around and looked right up into Ryan's dancing eyes.

"Oh," she fumbled, "I thought it was a mosquito."

"You're wearing repellent, remember?" he teased.

"Too bad they don't make Ryan Fox repellent," she bantered back, only to hear a chorus of "oohs" coming from the two men she had been talking to.

"Watch it, fellas, the pen is mightier than the tongue," she warned, and the men pretended to look contrite. "Better," she said with a laugh. "Much better."

"C'mon," Ryan urged, taking her by the arm. "I've had enough of crowds for a while."

"This from a baseball player?" she marveled as she let herself be led along.

"Especially from a baseball player." He didn't stop walking until they had gone quite a distance, almost out of sight of the others. He stopped by a tree, and Dallas found herself neatly maneuvered against the trunk. "Sometimes we just need to get away."

"Well, then—" she began to leave "—don't let me intrude on your solitude."

He caught her by her arm, pinning her again. "You're the reason I want solitude. You can't keep running forever."

The moment had turned suddenly serious. "I wasn't aware that I was running." Her voice was cool as she looked away.

He raised her chin with his fingertips until she was forced to look at him. "Then be aware. You're running. You have to touch base sometime."

She pressed her lips together. She didn't like the direction the conversation was taking, so she tried another topic. "You looked pretty comfortable out there with all those kids."

"I've got five brothers," he told her, his arms on either side of her forming a prison. "Between them, they've made me an uncle thirteen times over. I love kids."

"They seem to think the world of you, too."

His voice was low and husky. She felt his breath along her cheek as he lowered his head. "What do you think?"

"I think I'd like another soda," she answered breezily.

"Later."

"But I'm thirsty," she protested, unconsciously licking her lips.

He felt a tightening in the pit of his stomach again. "So am I."

She caught her breath just before he kissed her. If she hadn't been pressed against the tree she would have lost her balance. She curled her fingers around his arms to steady herself.

"You kiss like you pitch," she murmured. "Faster than the speed of light."

"I didn't want to give you time to protest," he said, leaning his forehead against hers. "Dallas?"

"Yes?" It was a breathless whisper, even though she tried to sound calm. But what was the use of trying to hide her arousal from him? He had been there to hear her breath shortening, to feel her heart pounding against him. She couldn't keep her reaction to him a secret anymore.

"Take a walk with me," he urged.

She looked back uncertainly in the direction of the party. "It wouldn't be polite—"

"No, what wouldn't be polite is if you let me go on suffering this way. I want to kiss you, Dallas, really kiss you, without risking being beaned by a ball, or asked to go another inning."

"I thought the kids were great?"

"They are. But so are you." He rubbed his face along her neck, igniting fires that should have been left alone. She knew she should say no, knew she should run for her life back to the security of the party.

She also knew she had no choice as she let him take her hand and lead her away.

Seven

Nothing had ever felt so right to Dallas as having her hand in his right now. She had no idea where Ryan was leading her; she only knew that she had to go, had to be with him, had to savor this one afternoon and then put him out of her mind. There was no place in her life for him. Her heart was ripe for giving, but she didn't want it to go to a ballplayer who would take her love, then throw it away.

Everything was so confusing. Things were happening much too fast. She wanted a relationship, so in one way Ryan had shown up at exactly the right time. But he was the wrong person.

He would mean heartbreak. She knew all the pressures, all the jealousies, all the problems that went along with marriage to a baseball star, and she wasn't going to let herself fall into the trap. She was too smart for that.

So how smart is it to play with fire? she mused, even as she felt the match being struck.

"Any particular destination in mind, or do we just keep on walking until we drop from exhaustion?" she asked, trying desperately to keep her excitement out of her voice.

He turned to her, his eyes mirroring the desire she felt. The crowds had long since disappeared. They were totally surrounded by trees, the brown earth carpeted with pine needles instead of grass, the sunlight overhead struggling to get through. They were alone.

"This'll do," he told her.

"Okay," she answered lightly. "We're here. Now what?"

He let go of her hand and raked his fingers through her hair, thinking he had never felt anything so soft. "Now I kiss you."

Her heart pounded in her throat. "You already kissed me."

The corners of his eyes crinkled. "Always being contrary."

"That depends on whose side you're on," she murmured as he moved his face closer to hers.

"I'm on yours," he whispered just before his lips touched hers.

No you're not, she thought, fighting a losing battle to keep seeing him as a bad guy in the black Stetson.

Her response was instantaneous, intense, as if his
very touch had detonated an incendiary device within
her. The explosion frightened her. Something name-
less, overpowering, frightening, was in control of her.
She found herself clinging to him, responding with an
intensity that surprised them both, an intensity that
turned his kiss passionate before the gentleness had a
chance to fade away.

He slid his hands along her hips, pressing her to him
as their bodies yearned to meld into a single form.

An insistent pull in her belly made her body de-
mand more. She was at once both languid and alert,
dazed, yet completely focused on the moment. She felt
as if she were being pulled in a thousand directions, as
sensation built upon sensation.

He savored her breath, sweet, urgent, as his mouth
moved over hers again and again. He had meant to
restrain himself, to sample a little more deeply of what
he knew was in store for him, but no more. Her response heightened his desire until he felt that there was
no turning back. Logic fled as he moved his hand under her breast, gently reaching for the single tie that
held her halter together.

Something tugged at the edge of her consciousness,
and she moved her hand up in protest. "No," she
murmured against his mouth. "Someone will see."

"I'll see," he whispered back, his words echoing
into her mouth.

Her fragile protest dissipated into nothing. The
touch of his rough, callused hand against her tender

skin aroused her. When he lowered his head to kiss her breast beneath the thin fabric she couldn't stop him, couldn't stop herself from wanting him. She pressed his head against her, closing her eyes and gliding along the crest of a feeling so pure, so devastating, that it almost numbed her.

He knew that in a moment he would lose the control he so cherished, would lose himself in the smell, the taste, the warmth, of her. With a superhuman effort he pulled back, wondering if she knew how much it took out of him to do so.

Her lids fluttered open, confusion in her bright green eyes.

"Not here," he told her.

"Thank you." She swallowed, fighting to regain her composure. How do you compose yourself in front of someone who's seen you gasping with passion? she wondered, trying with all her might not to admit to herself what had almost just happened, trying to deny the raw hunger that had taken hold and was only now subsiding, trying to deny the total loss of control she had experienced for the first time in her life.

"But soon," he promised. "Very, very soon."

"I'm afraid—"

He put his finger to her lips. "Don't be afraid," he told her. "When I make love to you, I intend to do it very, very gently."

She straightened, summoning the strength she had developed over the years. She began edging her way back toward the cookout. "If that day ever comes—" she began.

"It will," he interjected softly, following her. It has to, he thought. I've never felt so strongly about anyone before.

She pushed on. "*If* that day ever comes, you'll make love *with* me, not *to* me."

He grinned, and she melted. "Anything to oblige."

"There's a difference," she insisted.

He stopped walking and turned her around so that she was forced to look into his eyes again. "Yes," he said softly. "There is."

Did he really understand? She didn't know how to take his words, but was afraid to ask him to explain. They couldn't get serious about each other, whatever happened. She couldn't afford to let it happen. At most she should just enjoy each moment for what it was, a moment of pleasure. She couldn't think of a future with him, no matter how much she wanted one.

She turned away. "They'll be looking for us."

"That was one of the two things that stopped me." He took her hand, and they began walking again.

"And what was the other?"

"I hate pine needles."

She laughed, grateful for the shift in mood.

The barbecue lasted until dusk. Although there was no curfew that night a lot of the players had things they wanted to see to before they flew out the next day for Denver. They would be playing a three-game series with the Kings, and every game counted now.

Dallas remained silent during the long ride home. She rested her head against the back of the seat and closed her eyes, trying to relax. She couldn't, and hoped that he wasn't able to tell just how unsettled he made her feel, how totally susceptible she had become to him.

As he pulled into her driveway Dallas straightened, surprised. Her car was there.

"I always come through." Ryan grinned. "Sometimes it just takes a little longer, that's all."

"Just in time for me to leave it at the airport," she said glibly as she opened the car door.

"I can take you to the airport," he offered.

"No." She shook her head. "I think there's been a little too much togetherness between us. I wouldn't want the other players to get jealous." She laughed lightly, for a moment returning to her old self.

Her laughter made him think of the sound of the wind playing with the chimes that hung outside his mother's kitchen window. Light, silvery. It brought a wave of nostalgia washing over him. "That's their problem," he said.

"No," she said in a hushed tone. "It's ours." She licked her lips; he had noticed her doing it earlier when she was nervous and attempting to hide it. "Well, it was an interesting day, but I've still got that story to put to bed, not to mention myself."

Ryan put his hand over hers as she fumbled with her keys. "I'd like to come in, Dallas."

She took a breath to steady herself. "Yes, I know you would."

His eyes held hers. "Are you going to let me?"

She wavered. There was a war going on inside her, and she was afraid that she knew which side was going to win. There was nothing in his favor except her own raging desire, but that felt like more than enough.

"What do you think?"

"I think yes."

She pretended to be piqued. "I hate a man who's always right."

"We'll work on that," he promised as he took her arm and escorted her in.

It looked just the way he had thought it would, he decided, glancing around her living room. Clean, bright, with a smattering of baseball souvenirs from her father's day. It spoke of order and sudden fits of energy. It spoke of her.

"Can I get you anything?" she asked, fidgeting with the hem of her halter. "A beer? she added when he looked at her with an expectant look and a slightly boyish smile on his lips.

"Yes, please."

He made himself comfortable on the sofa. She thought, as she walked into the kitchen, that he looked as if he belonged there, as if he had been sitting there since the very beginning. In just a few days she had become accustomed to having him near. It was as if she were crowding a lifetime into the space of a few days.

And that's what you'll get out of this, she told herself. A few days, a few fleeting days. And then comes the off-season, when he has nothing to do and you're off covering football. How are you going to keep the relationship alive then? And what about the future? He'll probably switch teams again and go his own way, and you'll go yours, with nothing to remind you that you've touched except for an incredible ache inside you. I can't let it happen! she thought fiercely, afraid of letting go, afraid of feeling anything for him for more than a few seconds at a time.

She marched out of the kitchen. "Here."

She stuck the can of beer into his hand so abruptly that she startled him. He had been looking at a framed picture of her and her father. She looked to have been about fifteen. He couldn't help wondering what she had been like then.

He eyed the can she had slapped into his hand. "Is it safe to drink?"

She stood over him, her hands on her hips, impatience outlining every feature. Why had she let him in? "What are you talking about?"

"You just shoved that at me as if your mother told you that you had to be nice to me. I thought maybe you'd put a little poison in it," he joked.

Instinctively he knew he had struck the wrong cord with his careless comment. Her face tightened, as if he had just awakened a painful memory she wasn't prepared for. "My mother never told me anything." Her voice was suddenly very hollow. "Not even good-bye."

He set the beer down on the coffee table and rose, taking her into his arms. She resisted, but he wouldn't let her wrestle away. "I'm sorry. That was a very, very poor choice of words."

Dallas shrugged, trying to appear indifferent. "I take it Rusty told you?"

"Yes."

"How much?"

"Just that she left and your father started taking you with him on the road."

She nodded, and he could see her expression soft-ening. "He could have left me with my grandmother. It would have been easier for him. But he didn't. It wasn't easy being a single parent in those days, espe-cially not a single male parent with a baseball career. But he never wanted me to feel alone." Suddenly her eyes clouded over with a haze of tears, but she forced them back. "I'm being overly sensitive. I'm sorry, too." She looked at him accusingly. "But you have a habit of doing that to me."

"What?" He drew the word out softly, as if coax-ing a child to go on with a painful explanation.

"Making me feel vulnerable, making me feel as if something is missing."

"It is."

She raised her chin defiantly. "Oh? And what is that?"

He held her tighter. "Me."

It was her undoing. She had no one to blame except herself. She had let him come in; she had let him touch her heart in a way no one else ever had. "Ryan?" she asked hesitantly, unable to stop herself.

"Yes?"

"Do you want to kiss me again?"

With the tip of his finger he outlined her lips, then watched them tremble beneath his touch. "More than I want to breathe."

"Then stop talking and do it." Before I lose my nerve, she added silently.

Her take-charge attitude intermingled with her vulnerability made her so unique and so desirable that he thought his need for her would explode if he couldn't have her. And soon.

As his lips met hers, she could feel both fear and desire welling up within her. His mouth moved unhurriedly against hers in a slow, tantalizing dance, turning her body into sweet fire. She didn't know what had come over her. No other man had ever affected her this way, actually making her a stranger to herself.

Ryan felt Dallas's heart beat faster as his mouth left her lips and grazed the hollow of her throat. Dallas tilted her head back in an unconscious request for more. With agonizing persistence his kisses fluttered along her skin. From the hollow of her throat to her collarbone, then finally along her skin to the point where her top was tied. She shivered as she felt him loosen the bow. Very gently he exposed one breast. Softly he ran the back of his hand against it.

And then he stopped abruptly. She opened her eyes, silently asking him why.

"My hands are callused. I might hurt you." She suddenly looked very frail and delicate to him.

Dallas placed her hand over his and drew it back wordlessly, mute supplication in her eyes.

Deeply aroused, he kissed her lips again, his hand taking possession of her and stroking her so gently that she thought she would scream. His tongue probed, tasted, drained all the sweetness in her mouth. Dallas wound her hands around his neck, pressing herself closer to him as if to warm herself in the fire he was creating. She was suddenly very cold, and she needed his heat.

He did nothing but kiss and stroke her for what seemed like an eternity, and she felt both a tranquility and a restlessness that she didn't know how to deal with. She wanted him to make love with her, wanted that wild, torrid moment that waited at the end of all this, but that would mean the end was at hand, and she was always afraid of the end. No, she didn't want to give up the feelings that were ripping through her body now. She wanted them to last forever.

She thought she was floating, then realized that he had pushed her back until she rested on the floor, her hair fanned out against the deep brown rug, her body pinned beneath his.

"We'll go slow," he promised, seeing the uncertain look in her eyes.

Not too slow, she pleaded silently. I don't know if I could stand it.

Ryan pulled her halter entirely away and showered kisses along her other breast until she moaned with pleasure, sinking her teeth into her lip to keep from crying out.

A last-moment panic seized her even though she knew she faced the inevitable, craved the inevitable. "Ryan," she cried.

He lifted his head, his deep blue eyes studying her face. "Yes?"

"I don't..." She swallowed the words.

"But you will," he whispered against her mouth.

And then she couldn't say anything at all. His kiss, soft, gentle, deep, stole all her words from her, all her thoughts, all shreds of sanity. She needed this, needed *him*. She had known somehow from the very first moment she saw him that he was trouble, that he would change her life the way no one else had even come close to doing.

Her body moved beneath him without her consent, without any thought. She was his to do with as he would, to take her to a place where she had never been.

She felt him move to shift her shirt from beneath her and vaguely heard him ask her to sit up. When she did Ryan replaced the fabric with whisper-soft kisses. Gently he pushed her back as his kisses surged on, a demanding, relentless army covering the terrain and conquering everything in its path.

Her stomach muscles quivered as his tongue circled her navel. In an instant the snap that held her shorts had been released and she felt him sliding her shorts down her long legs. The heel of his hand pressed against the triangle of flesh that lay beneath her cotton panties, warm, moist and wanting, massaging it until she was all but mindless. She reached for him, pulled him to her and took his mouth with a fierceness she hadn't known she was capable of.

He knew there was no holding back any longer. He wanted this to be special for her; it was special to him, but the demands of his body and her response wrenched control from him. He stripped off his jersey quickly, then cast it aside on the floor.

Dallas watched through a haze as he shed his jeans. The sight of his muscular, taut body caused something to sizzle within her.

"Now, Ryan," she said hoarsely, not thinking of the fact that her plea would embarrass her later. "Now."

He cradled her in his arm, his free hand stroking her from her hip to her breast and then back again. "No, not yet, darlin'," he whispered, his drawl as heavy as her limbs. "Just a little longer."

He explored every inch of her body with a slowness that gave her no hint of the passion that churned demandingly within his loins. He wanted to know her, know her fully. Though he was unable to understand the fear that he saw in her eyes, he was determined to at least understand the workings of her body. He wanted to bring her to a fever pitch such as she had never felt before. He wanted, he realized, to matter to her, to be special.

With deft movements, strategic kisses and touches that soothed and stimulated at the same time he unlocked the secrets of her body. Dallas arched her back, pulling him to her, kissing him with a hunger that finally broke his control. He rolled on top of her, but at first did nothing more than kiss her mouth over and over while their bodies grew hotter with longing and the knowledge of what lay just ahead. And then, as he raised himself slightly on his elbows, he looked at her for a long moment, then curled his tongue inside her ear before he spoke.

"Guide me," he whispered, his body shuddering with need.

"I don't know how." The words squeezed themselves out and she looked to the side.

He stopped kissing her. "You never...?"

"No." She looked away.

He turned her face back to his with his fingertips. "This puts a new light on things," he whispered. He moved off her and his hand went back to the silken core of her femininity and with patient, gentle strokes he made her ready to receive him.

Dallas moved with each stroke, rising to the insistent heat he roused in her. Then he rolled onto her again, and she felt the urgent press of his hot, throbbing body as it called to hers.

"This may hurt," he warned her gently. "But I'll be careful. I promise."

"I . . . don't . . . care. . . ."

She felt a throaty laugh ripple through him. "You're beautiful, Dallas," he told her just before he entered.

She winced a little, but the heat of his mouth over hers seared away the pain and brought with it flashes of electricity and a sensation so overwhelming that it had no beginning, no end.

She felt his sweat mingling with hers, and then she was launched into a world of brilliant sensations as he moved with growing intensity inside her. She tried vainly to gather every feeling to her, to hold it tightly, but then a new one would break and she found herself gasping, clinging, crying with the wonder of what she was experiencing.

The sound of his breathing growing louder excited her even when she felt she could stand no more. She clung to him, finally realizing that she loved him. It was the last thought that streaked across her mind before a heavy peacefulness blanketed her body and she let out a gasp, then fell, safe and warm, into the oblivion that reached up to claim her.

Slowly she became aware of a weight on her. Ryan had slid slightly to the side, but his arms were still around her, his head still against the soft curve of her neck.

He felt her rouse and lifted his head. "Hi." His smile was soft, and warmth curled in the pit of her stomach.

"Hi, yourself," she murmured lazily, waiting for embarrassment to claim her. Nothing happened. Nothing disturbed her feeling of euphoria.

Ryan propped himself on his elbow, drawing her closer. "You didn't tell me you were a virgin."

"It never worked its way into the conversation. It's stamped with invisible ink on my union card, though."

Banter. She was hiding behind banter again. For now he would let her seek its safety, but there was one more question nagging him. "Why...?" he began.

"Because."

He began playing with a strand of her hair, bringing it to his lips and kissing it softly. "I can't believe no one ever tried."

She smiled. "I never wanted anyone to try. And my dad was a big man. No one was going to force himself on Champ's daughter if he had any brains."

"I would have," he volunteered. Slowly he began stroking her breast, teasing her senses awake again.

"Maybe you don't have any brains."

"Maybe," he said softly. "But I know what I *do* have."

"What?"

"An incredible desire to kiss you again."

"What are you going to do about it?"

"Give in."

She reached out to him, still under the spell of what had just happened. "Sounds good to me."

Eight

They made love two more times that night. Each time was more exquisite than the last. Finally, without a shred of energy left between them, they fell asleep in each other's arms.

Sometime before dawn Ryan woke up, a warm shape curled against him. He opened his eyes and saw her. A thoughtful smile slipped over his lips as he reached out and softly stroked her hair.

Dallas murmured something in her sleep and snuggled into the pocket formed by his body and the mattress.

Without her barbs and sharp tongue and the wary look in her eyes, she looked so innocent. Watching her sleep, seeing her face wreathed in rosy innocence, he felt a pang in his heart. It startled him.

Very quietly he eased himself out of bed.

Dallas had no idea what woke her, whether it was a dream or the need to touch him once more, to assure herself that he was there. With her eyes still closed she reached out for him—and touched nothing.

Sleep faded and she opened her eyes. The bed was empty. The sheets beneath her hand felt cold, as if he hadn't been there for some time.

"Ryan?" she called, sitting up.

There was no answer.

Slowly she raised her head. Her expression turned from confusion to something far more somber. The bathroom door was open, but he wasn't in there.

Nude, she left her bed and grabbed a robe from her closet. She pushed her arms through the sleeves as she made her way from the bedroom to the kitchen, a growing uncertainty gnawing at her stomach.

The kitchen was empty. From where she stood she could look into the living room. She saw the sofa where he had seemed to fit so well only twelve hours ago.

His clothes were gone.

Dallas's lip curled in contempt as anger replaced hurt. "I underestimated you, Fox. Even I didn't think you'd leave this fast."

* * *

She stripped her bed in search of a note. There had to be a note. He couldn't be that cruel, could he? She had thought she was beginning to know him. Could she have been so wrong, so foolish, and given herself for the first time to a man with no heart?

There was no note.

Slowly she managed to work her hurt into something she could deal with, something she could live with: plain bitterness. But that didn't stop her from hoping that the phone would ring.

She wanted the satisfaction of hanging up on him when he presented her with his paltry excuse, she told herself as she slapped clothes into the suitcase that lay open on her bed. She had a plane to catch.

A plane he would be on. But that, she told Fish crisply as she stormed into the kitchen, couldn't be helped. There were forty other players to cover, and she was a professional. There was no time for her to sit around and nurse hurt feelings.

"Hurt? Hell, they're scarred." She tossed extra flakes into Fish's blow. "But I'll get over it. If he thinks I'm going to moon over him then he's a bigger jerk than I thought he was. First impressions, Fish, are always right. Stick with them."

Except, a small voice reminded her, her real first impression of him had been something other than the one she had voiced. Her first impression of him had zinged a bolt of electricity through her.

"So he causes electrical storms in women. In my book, Fish, his name is M-U-D."

She had to face three days in Denver. Three days in which the Rebels had to win two games in order to knock out the competition. For that, she knew, she would have to root for Ryan at least once. He was the starting pitcher for the second game. Well, baseball made strange alliances.

Muttering a curse, Dallas slammed her front door behind her and locked it. As she walked to her car she paused to look around.

"Idiot, are you waiting for him to show up? He got what he wanted. He played another perfect game, sliding home where no one's ever batted a run before. Now he's got other games to play."

But not even she, in her darkest assessment of him, would have thought that he would leave in the middle of the night without a single word.

Why? The question haunted her during her trip to the airport.

She got to the freeway exit in record time, only to get bogged down in heavy traffic just a mile from the airport. Finally she got there, but she had to pass terminal after terminal until she arrived at the parking lot. Jockeying for position, she signaled insistently and jammed her car in front of a navy-blue Seville. The color reminded her of Ryan's eyes.

"Damn it, Dallas, get hold of yourself," she muttered. Finally she parked, then walked angrily around to the trunk and opened it. She pulled out her suitcase and simultaneously pasted a chipper look on her face. If she was going to run into Ryan, she wanted to look as if nothing had happened, as if she were totally and blissfully unaware of anything amiss. In short, as if she didn't give a tinker's damn that he had left her bed without so much as a word or, she surmised, a backward glance.

Once inside the terminal, she spotted Jawersky. She waved, and he waited, giving her a chance to catch up to him. They stepped on the escalator together.

She steadied herself by grabbing the moving handrail. "I've been meaning to do a column on you."

"I'd say it's about time, honey." He gave her what he deemed to be his most beguiling smile.

The woods were full of them, she thought wryly, getting a fix on her feelings. "Jawersky," she began with a hint of humor in her eyes, "you're a Harvard grad. There's no reason for you to sound as if you're some hotshot lover coming on to me."

Jewersky slipped a heavy arm around her shoulders. "At least with my superior education I can see exactly why the Fox is so interested in you."

"The Fox," she said lightly, neatly returning his arm to him, "is off trying to raid another hen house. Now, I thought we might get started right after the game."

"Why wait?" He grinned at her broadly. "We could get started right away. I'll have McGee's seat switched and we could get real cozy—"

"No, we couldn't," she answered in a cheery voice, walking off the escalator first. Dallas was beginning to think that all the players spent their off hours trying to get to first base with women. Always keeping in practice, she thought with a bittersweet smile.

"Hiya, good lookin'." She turned, relieved to hear Rusty's voice. "What's going on?" He joined them, looking rather suspiciously at the tall, broad-shouldered third-baseman.

"I think I just fouled out," Jawersky told Rusty honestly.

"Pop fly over the dugout," Dallas confirmed.

"There'll be other times at bat," Jawersky said confidently. Just at that moment a curvaceous blonde walked by, obviously alone. "Hmmm. Excuse me." He turned and walked away.

Even Jawersky excused himself before he left, Dallas thought. A resurgence of bitterness claimed her.

"Catch you later," the big ballplayer called over his shoulder as he set his sights on the blonde.

Rusty put his arm around Dallas and led her to the cluster of seats by their gate. "You've gotta watch out for these wolves, Dallas."

Dallas sat down. "As far as I'm concerned it's the Foxes that are lethal, not the wolves."

Rusty eyed her. "You and Foxy have a fight?"

"Not exactly," she said evasively.

"Just what did go down, 'exactly'?"

She smiled, patting his cheek fondly. "You're not my father, Rusty."

"I'm not trying to measure up to the Champ; I'm just kind of looking after his girl."

Dallas looked around the crowded waiting area, absently wondering where all these people were going. "His girl is all grown up and very capable of handling her own affairs." She winced, suddenly realizing her Freudian slip.

Rusty's brows knitted together as he tried to determine if he were reading her words correctly. "Dallas, did he, um, you know, get out of line?"

She shrugged. "It all depends on where he thought the line was drawn."

"You're going to keep me guessing, aren't you?"

She merely nodded, a trace of her humor returning. And then her expression froze. She saw Ryan in the distance. He was standing by himself near the huge bay window, watching the planes go by.

Rusty looked over and saw Ryan. "I don't think I'm guessing anymore. Something *did* go wrong last night, didn't it?"

"You might say that," she answered crisply. "If you'll excuse me—" she rose "—I think I'll get started on my column early." She looked around and saw that Jawersky was standing by himself. The previous object of his attention was now surrounded by three small children and a very husky husband. Jawersky saw Dallas looking and he shrugged his shoulders sheepishly.

Dallas laughed. "Hey, Jawersky!" She joined the third-baseman before Rusty could say anything further.

Ryan saw Dallas's reflection in the glass as he looked out. He watched her covertly, trying, for the first time in his life, to summon courage. Courage wasn't a thing he thought about very much; it was just something that was there. It took guts and courage to put your dreams on the line, and he had done it without a single thought. He had given himself one summer to make it from the minors to the majors or quit, and he had made it.

But early this morning, in the predawn light, his courage had flagged. An unnamed, icy panic had set in when he realized that he might have found just what he had said he was looking for. He had found a woman he could love, a woman he wanted to spend the rest of his days with. And it had frightened the hell out of him. His emotions in a jumble, for the first time in his life he had acted irrationally. He had left to clear his head. He couldn't think around her. All he could do was want her. Three times he had made love to her last night, and it hadn't been enough, not nearly enough. He couldn't satisfy his desire for her, his desire or his need. It was as if each time he had her, he wanted more, much more. He had gotten as close to her physically as was possible, yet he felt there was still a barrier between them. No matter how passionately she gave her body to him, there was something more,

something that he didn't understand, something that
still kept her from being completely his.

And he wanted all of her even while he wavered
about giving her all of himself in return.

She had said it wasn't going to be simple, and she
had been right. Oh, so right, he thought.

He turned around and saw the way Jawersky's face
lit up as he talked to her. Another unaccustomed feeling took hold in him. He had never been jealous before, had never cared enough to be jealous. Yet now
he wanted to walk up to her and pull her away from
that overeducated, leering bastard.

That would be the fastest way to break negotiations with her, he thought. And there were going to
have to be negotiations. Only after he had gotten behind the wheel of his car that morning had he thought
about what waking up alone might do to her. He was
going to have to do some explaining—to both of them.

She certainly doesn't look upset now, he thought.

"Flight seven for Denver loading at gate number
five," an attendant announced over a loudspeaker, his
statement punctuated with static.

Ryan turned and went through to the plane.

Maybe it was for the best, Dallas thought as she sat
in the Denver Kings' press box and watched as
Thompson, a relief pitcher, stood on the mound,
sweating out the bottom of the ninth in the artificial
light. Ryan hadn't tried to approach her during the
flight, and her hotel phone had rung only once when
Jawersky called to ask if she wanted to grab a quick

bite to eat and continue the interview. She had said yes to the bite, yes to the interview, and no to the half-serious proposition that followed dessert. She thought now that maybe Ryan had more brains than she did, calling a halt to things before they got out of hand.

Got out of hand? Hell she was already dealing with a runaway team of horses with the reins dragging on the ground. It was too late to worry about the situation getting out of hand.

She forced her mind back to her work. Things on the field were in a sad state if you were rooting for the Rebels. They needed two more games to wrap up the western division championship, and things weren't going well tonight. After seven runs in three innings, they had stalled, watching as the Kings gained. Now the score was tied. Caldwell had been relieved in the sixth after giving away seven runs. Ryan, she knew, was in the dugout, probably pacing. Each game was important to him, whether he got to pitch or not.

Thompson walked the batter, and Howell Johnson came up to bat. The man was two for two. Dallas held her breath. If Thompson walked him the bases would be loaded. The pitcher was relatively new, having come up to the majors only last season. He was good, but right now he was visibly nervous, even from this distance. Dallas closed her eyes and prayed.

There was the sound of wood cracking.

"My God, look at that ball fly! It's a home run, folks!"

Dallas opened her eyes as the announcer's voice echoed in the press box. She wore a tight smile as she watched two reporters down front slap each other on the back. The home team had won the first game of the three-game series hands down.

Dallas gathered her papers and began to walk out. It was late, and she was tired. Maybe she would have room service send up a sandwich and call it a night. The last thing she wanted to do was write an article. There would be time enough for that in the morning. She was blessed with a talent that allowed her to piece together first drafts that carried the polish of a finished piece.

Loyalty took her down to the locker room instead. She stood outside, waiting, until one by one the players, showered, changed and sobered, filed out. "Tomorrow," she said to a couple of them. "We'll get 'em tomorrow."

"One-girl cheering section, aren't you?" Rusty asked fondly as he emerged from the locker room. "No, excuse me, Foxy said to call you a woman."

Dallas immediately forgot how tired she was. "How's that again?"

"He said if anyone deserved the title of woman, it was you," Rusty said, remembering Ryan's exact words when they had first discussed Dallas.

"Oh, he did, did he?" she asked slowly, her anger and hurt beginning to flare. He had talked about last night to Rusty. What other possible explanation was there for what Rusty had just said? How dare he make her the topic of locker room talk! What that hit-and-run Casanova needed was for someone to put him in his place. And she was just the one to do it, she told herself.

Dallas squared her shoulders and pushed the locker room door open.

"Hey, I thought you didn't go into locker rooms," Rusty called after her, surprised.

"I'm changing my image," she retorted without looking back.

There was no one left except Ryan. He had purposely waited for the others to go because tonight he wanted to be alone, wanted to divorce himself from the quasi-family situation that a team bred. He was still trying to put his feelings in order. That, coupled with the fact that the pressure would be on him tomorrow to win the game, made him want his solitude.

He was surprised to see her. He was even more surprised to see the angry look on her face.

"Bastard," she said as she slammed down her clipboard on the bench.

She narrowly missed hitting him as he jumped back. "I didn't pitch today," he protested, knowing how she felt about the Rebels.

"No, but you sure did last night," she snapped, her eyes blazing.

An awkward feeling washed over him. "Oh, that."

"Yes, that. Maybe I shouldn't be angry. It could have been worse," she fumed. "You could have left a five dollar bill on the bureau."

He was on his feet, confused. "What are you talking about?"

"You treated me worse than some two-bit bimbo you picked up on the road."

"I don't pick up two-bit bimbos," he said angrily.

"Excuse me, four-bits then," she spat out. "And then to talk about it to Rusty! I don't know why I'm wasting my time here. I—I—" She ran out of breath and out of words. Furious, she spun on her heel and stalked out.

Ryan jumped over the bench that was in his way and leaped in front of her, blocking her exit. "I don't know what you're talking about. I didn't talk to anyone, and I left for two reasons."

She averted her face, afraid that if she looked at him she would lose hold of the anger she felt. "I don't care to hear them."

"The hell you don't." He grabbed her wrists, preventing her from leaving. "If you didn't, you wouldn't have stormed in here looking like a hurricane about to happen." He took a deep breath. "I left because I didn't want to see the look of regret in your eyes when you woke up."

His answer stopped her. "What?"

"Regret," he repeated. "I didn't want you to be sorry for what happened between us. And," he went on, his voice growing lower, "I panicked."

"What's that supposed to mean?"

"It means that things are happening too fast, and I don't know if I'm seeing all this in the right light, or if I'm creating something in my mind because I've wanted a good relationship for so long."

He let go of her wrists and touched her hair. Even in the dim locker room light he could see the shining highlights. He wanted to bury his face in it, inhale its perfume deeply. "This is all very new to me."

"Is that a line?" she asked uncertainly, wanting to believe him, yet afraid. For a dozen reasons.

He shook his head. "I never use lines. Ask Rusty."

"You bring him along on many dates?" she asked.

He didn't bother answering. "I'm sorry."

"Oh God, don't be nice to me. I wanted to have your head on a platter; let me leave it that way."

"No, I can't. I won't. I know what's frightening me, Dallas." He took her by the shoulders, the pressure of his fingers gentle but firm. "But I don't know what's frightening you."

She looked into his eyes, aware that everything in the room was fading rapidly away. "You," she answered.

"Why?"

"You represent everything I always said I didn't want. And yet I do."

"I don't understand."

"I'm not sure I do, either."

He kissed her lips. "Then let's find the answer together. Let me help you, Dallas."

She didn't want this, she thought, struggling with her rising passion. She didn't want a relationship with a baseball hero, especially one whose attitude was so unlike her father's. A man like Ryan, whose attitude went against everything she held dear.

But she felt her resistance, her anger, fading. "I don't need help. I need willpower."

"Why?"

"To keep me from melting every time you kiss me."

"That," he said between covering her mouth with small, arousing kisses, "I won't help you find."

Nine

He was doing it to her again. He was making love to her senses, and she had to stop him before it went too far. With an effort Dallas put her hands against Ryan's chest and pushed. She had to create some space between them. Being pressed up against him robbed her of her good sense. "Ryan, someone might come in."

He cupped her face in his hands, running his thumb along her lower lip. "The clean-up crew isn't due for hours, and the last guy left. We're alone. We can do anything we please." He ran his finger along her chin.

Dallas checked a shudder. "What about curfew?"

"Don't worry about it." Feathery kisses touched her temples. "They won't come down on me. They need me tomorrow. Besides, you're worth any penalty."

Dallas sighed deeply as her senses began to swim. "You've got to stop saying things like that. I just might believe you," she said wryly, knowing that she already *did* believe him, at least in her heart. "And after what you did last night..."

His breath caressed her cheek as he held her tightly against him, his body romancing hers. "I thought I explained all that." For a moment he held her at arm's length. His dark eyes searched hers. Yes, he could detect a trace of suspicion there. Or were those his own uncertainties reflected in her face? "You don't believe all that nonsense you've seen in print, do you? You of all people should know better than to believe everything you read."

"I don't believe everything I read, but you have to admit you did act exactly the way I might have expected you to if I *did* believe those articles about your being a playboy." Uncertainty lingered in her mind even as she tried to argue it away. "But that's not the whole problem."

He sat down on the bench and pulled her onto his lap. "Then what is?" He locked his hands around her waist.

She didn't like being put on the spot this way. She, who had always been taught to speak her mind, now couldn't find the right words. She stared at a jagged crack in the dull green wall in front of her. She didn't trust herself to look directly into his eyes, and hated herself for being a coward. "Ryan, maybe you were right. Maybe this is all happening too fast. Maybe we should take a breather."

He said nothing, merely waited for her to go on. They needed to explore their innermost feelings as much as they needed to explore each other physically.

The locker room, so alive with sounds and smells a short half hour ago, now stood like a silent tomb. A tomb, she thought. How fitting considering all the feelings she kept buried in her heart.

Finally she turned away from the wall and looked into his face, really looked at him. She wanted to see beyond the raw good looks. She wanted to see what was inside his head, how he really felt and what he really thought. There was much more to him than appeared on the surface. If she could understand him, then maybe this would work.

Maybe.

"You're waiting for an explanation," she finally said. "I don't know if I can give it to you."

"Try."

"It has a lot to do with what I've seen over the years. And my mother."

"Your mother?" It was the last thing he had expected her to say.

"She ran out on me, on us, my father and me. She ran out on a marriage to a baseball player because she couldn't stand the thought of his succumbing to the temptations on the road."

"How do you know that's how she felt?"

"My dad told me," she answered simply, though Ryan sensed that there was nothing simple about the revelation. "Not then, but when I grew up, when I could understand." She tried to make Ryan comprehend. "I don't want that to happen to me. To us."

He tilted her chin so he could reach her mouth. "It won't." Gently, lightly, he kissed her lips and her cheek. Despite all her efforts her frown changed into a smile.

But she refused to give in to the sensations he was arousing in her. "I've seen it time and again. What do you think makes us so different?" Then she regretted what she had said. Her question presupposed that he had a permanent relationship on his mind. It gave away her feelings, made her more vulnerable.

"Hadn't you noticed?" he murmured against her mouth, teasing her with his sweet breath. "We're special."

"Be serious," she pleaded, feeling herself weakening.

He nipped at her neck. "I intend to be."

"Ryan."

He stopped kissing her, checked by the serious tone in her voice. But he continued to hold her on his lap, his hands about her waist as if he were afraid that if he let her go she would take flight.

"Dallas, I can't give you any guarantees. I can't give me any guarantees, either. This is all pretty new to me, but I'm willing to take it one step at a time if you are."

She looked down at the scuffed floor. "I don't know if I can."

"Here," he whispered against the hollow of her neck. "Let me help you make up your mind."

She didn't stand a chance against both him and her own longings. He seemed so sincere, as confused as she was, but sincere. Maybe they had more in common than she thought. Maybe that was why she reacted so quickly to him, why she couldn't really resent him. There were kindred spirits.

All he had to do was kiss her and she felt herself melting against him, her body aflame with desires that he had awakened that first time on her doorstep.

It didn't matter that they were in a locker room, that any moment someone might walk in for a forgotten item, that a cleaning crew was due in a few hours. All that mattered was that he wanted her. She *needed* to be wanted, wanted by this man. She might have tried to reject him with words for what she felt were all the right reasons, but her body told him the truth. She wanted him. Oh, how she wanted him, she thought. He was the master of her passion, the key to her desires.

He could feel her anguish as much as he felt her passion. At a loss as to how to quell her doubts, how to make her fears vanish, all he could do was show her the extent of his love. That was what had panicked him in the wee hours of the morning, tightening his chest and wrenching his stomach. He loved her. And really loving someone brought a world of responsibilities, responsibilities that he now felt he could face.

He loved all the foibles and quirks that went into making her what she was. And it bothered him a great deal that she kept so many barriers between them in her mind when he was conquering his. He had always felt that anything worthwhile took time, so he had been surprised by the rapidity with which love had overtaken him. This, it seemed, was the price he had to pay: convincing her that she felt the same way, waiting out her problems so that she could return his feelings without fear.

He only had one weapon besides patience.

Dallas moved to the inner music he created as his tongue left a moist trail from the throbbing pulse at her throat to the valley between her breasts. She laced her fingers together behind his head and pressed him to her urgently, savoring the electricity he sent racing through her.

"This isn't fair," she managed to protest, her eyes half shut from the drugging effect his teasing mouth had on her. "You're fighting on home territory."

"You're the visitor," he pointed out. "The last time we played in your stadium."

"Played?" she managed to ask.

"Poor choice of words again," he apologized. "I'm a doer, not a talker." He caressed her breast as he spoke, taking pleasure in the fact that she couldn't endure his touch passively. "Not like Jawersky."

For the first time since she had entered the locker room he saw her smile. "He can talk, all right."

Ryan wondered just what it was that she and the third-baseman had talked about. "I take it you're much too bright to be taken in by anything he has to say."

He was jealous. The thought made her inexplicably happy. "Of course. For all his knowledge the man's as empty as a drive-in in the rain."

"I'd like to do that sometime," Ryan said as he caressed the area around her nipple. He saw it harden and strain through the light silk fabric. "Take in a drive-in movie with you and steam up the windows. I'd like to make love *with* you," he gave her a little nod to show he remembered her correction, "in the shower, taking my time and lathering every delicious inch of you." He gently stroked her other breast and heard her suppress a moan. "I'd like to do something out of the ordinary."

Her limbs felt heavy, and it took all the effort she could muster to keep from totally succumbing to his attack. "This isn't exactly your average run-of-the-mill place to make love." She gestured around the room, then took his face in her hands, drawing him away from her breasts. "Or is it?"

He took hold of her hands, kissing each upturned palm in turn. "I wouldn't know. I was a virgin until the other night."

"Like hell you were," she said, then laughed.

He rose, drawing her with him as he edged over to the whirlpool. "Let's just say that everything that came before has all blurred into a meaningless dream." He turned the whirlpool on and it began to hum. "Care for a little medicinal treatment?"

"That tub's only meant for one person at a time."

"I rise to challenges," he teased.

"Ryan . . ." She eyed the humming machine as the water began to froth and foam. "I really don't think—"

"Good," he whispered, coming up behind her, his breath warming her cheek. "Don't think. Let me do it for us."

She turned as he began unbuttoning her blouse. "This is crazy."

He grinned widely. "Doc Nelson highly recommends one of these things right after a stressful game."

"We haven't had a stressful game."

The blouse fell to the floor and he began working on the snap of her bra. "Give us time."

She felt as if she didn't have time, as if her heart was beating so hard that time meant nothing. She was aware only of the sensations he was creating as he stripped her of her clothes.

His kisses, small and light, grew longer and more intense as he nipped and sampled every possible area of her body, drawing responses from her that she'd had no idea she was capable of. In her haze she realized he was kneeling before her, sliding down her underwear and kissing her inch after titillatingly torturous inch. Her panties dropped to her ankles and she gasped, feeling his tongue weave a magic that took her breath away. She held on to his shoulders tightly, her nails digging in as he created stunning hot and cold flashes all through her by turns.

When she opened her eyes again she was surprised to see that he had removed his own clothing. She had no idea when or how; nothing was in its proper perspective.

"And now," he said, picking her up, "that soothing treatment I promised you."

She put her arms around his neck. "I think you're going about soothing me the wrong way."

He laughed softly against her neck. "Maybe."

The water was hot, but she hardly noticed. Her body was already on fire. She couldn't take her eyes off him. Last night she had been too consumed with the wonder of what was happening to really look. She looked now, taking in every detail: the smooth, muscular chest; the flat, taut stomach; the smattering of hair that curled about his navel, darkening as it descended.

"You're staring." He laughed, lowering himself into the tank. Water overflowed the sides.

"I know." She tried to shift to give him room and found that she could barely move.

"Didn't anyone ever teach you not to stare?"

She shook her head. She felt the delicious sensations of the bubbling waters and his inviting body at the same time, "I guess there are a lot of things I never learned."

"Don't worry." He smiled as his body moved against hers. "You're a quick study."

The look of desire in her eyes made him abandon his banter. He was only human, and he could deny the cries of his body only so long. Control had little to do with loving Dallas. Giving her pleasure only served to fuel his own passions, his own needs. He felt pleasure now as their bodies all but entwined in the pulsating water.

He kissed her lips, adoring the way her mouth opened for his tongue. He caressed her body beneath the water, pressing her hips against his.

She felt his arousal and her heart beat faster. "Are you going to warn me that this might hurt again?"

She was exceptional. How could he ever have worried that she might turn out like all the others? Dallas had style, had life, had laughter in her soul. And she had his heart in her hand. "Only if we blow up the machine."

"What are the chances of that happening?" she asked.

"I don't know. Let's see."

He began making love to her there and then, his smoldering passion hidden behind light words and teasing looks. Their first attempt at union brought near disastrous results. Dallas found herself slipping beneath the churning waters.

"Are you trying to make love to me or drown me?" she asked, resurfacing.

"Not doing a very good job of either one, am I?" He grinned despite himself. Tenderly he pushed her wet hair out of her eyes.

"No. This is going to take teamwork," she murmured. "Sit down."

With amusement and passion on his face he obeyed. She straddled him, and suddenly there was no more time for light words. He buried his head between her breasts as he filled her slowly, holding himself back as much as he dared, then beginning to move ever so slightly.

Dallas dug her fingers into his shoulders again. "I promise I won't breathe," she whispered against his shoulder, savoring the rapid way his heart was beginning to beat.

The rhythm of their movements increased until it matched the wildly surging foam on the water. Dallas hadn't thought that anything could match the power and majesty of last night. She had been wrong. Exquisite sensations peaked and flowered into other sensations that took her higher and higher to a summit she had not gained before, until the final explosion occurred.

And then the only movement was the churning of the water. Dallas clung to Ryan, euphoric happiness filling her.

"See?" He pushed the hair from her face lovingly. "Purely medicinal."

"I don't think I can trust you," she teased, kissing his mouth.

"Not if you start that again."

"Then maybe we'd better go." Her tone was regretful.

"All right, but don't think you've seen the last of me."

Dallas laughed and accepted his hand as she got out. She saw the look that entered Ryan's eyes as they swept over her.

"Let me get a towel and dry you," he offered.

"No," she protested. "You know where that would lead."

"Yes, that's why I volunteered."

"Later," she said, grabbing one of the towels stacked on the table behind them.

He watched her dry herself and hunger began again in his loins. "Promise?"

It was a voice full of all the soft, tender things she had always said she wanted. Never mind that it came from a man she felt couldn't deliver all he promised forever.

"Yes."

Rusty was outside the locker room saying goodbye to the last few fans when they came out ten minutes later. Dallas blushed, thinking how close they had come to being caught. Rusty looked chagrined, too, but Dallas suspected he was also pleased that she and Ryan had made up. He fell into step with them, and

Ryan put his arm around Dallas, hugging her close as they left the stadium. "Hey!" She glanced down at her watch. "We'd better hurry up. The witching hour is almost here. Gibson wouldn't want his star pitcher—"

"And star shortstop."

"And star shortstop," Dallas obliged, "out past curfew."

"What about 'later'?" Ryan asked, reminding her of her promise in the locker room.

Dallas smiled broadly. "Later is a relative term."

Ryan narrowed his eyes. "You're welshing, aren't you?"

"Fox," she said cheerfully as she unlocked the door of the rented car she had waiting, "I never welsh. Meet me after the game tomorrow." She winked flirtatiously.

"C'mon, Sullivan." Ryan put his hand on Rusty's shoulder. "The lady's just offered to take us back to the hotel."

Rusty looked back toward his own rental car, then waved his hand at it dismissively. He could always pick it up the next day. "Only if I drive."

Dallas smiled, handing him the keys as she looked at Ryan. "Care to join me in the back seat?" she asked with a smile.

Ryan laughed, and for a moment he pretended that the pressure wasn't on. Tomorrow he would outline his strategy against the Kings. Tonight he could only go over the fine details of making love to a beautiful woman in a whirlpool.

They rode back to the hotel in relative silence, Rusty doing the driving and most of the talking. Dallas was content just to lean back in Ryan's arms. The old nagging doubts were still there, but far in the background of her mind. Right now she wanted to savor the happiness she was experiencing. Who knew when it would all disappear?

When they arrived at the hotel Dallas let the doorman park the car. She rode up with Ryan and Rusty, listening to them talk about the next day's game and how it would be "a piece of cake," despite tonight's debacle.

"Hey, this is our room," Rusty called as Ryan walked right by it.

"Don't worry, I'll be back," Ryan promised, his arm possessively around Dallas's shoulders.

She turned at her door, which was down the hall. "Ryan, you can't come in. I won't let you. You need your rest for tomorrow. This is exactly why God made curfews." She put her hands against his chest to keep him at bay, but she couldn't help smiling as she did it.

Ryan sighed. "Trust Champion Carlyle's daughter to lecture me when all I want is to make love to her over and over again until I drop."

"You wouldn't do the Rebels any good tomorrow." She tried to keep a straight face.

"No, but I could do myself a hell of a lot of good tonight."

She grabbed the lapels of his shirt and brushed her lips against his. "Good night, Fox. I've got an article to write."

"If it's about Jawersky don't give his column as many words as you give mine."

She nodded solemnly. "Half." She crossed her heart.

"A quarter," he tossed over his shoulder as he went down the hall to his room.

"Didn't I say she was something else?" Rusty asked when Ryan walked into their room.

Ryan didn't even bother taking off his clothes. He stretched out on his bed, his hands tucked under his head. "That you did, Sullivan, that you did."

Rusty smiled to himself, wondering if Dallas would like to have him give her away.

Ten

─────

She had never been one to watch a baseball game impassively, even after her father had stopped playing. He had implanted a basic love of the sport in her from early on. As she matured Dallas had come to the conclusion that nowhere could the emotions of a crowd be so churned up as during a close baseball game. The tension in the air crackled like static electricity.

It was just like the way she felt when she and Ryan made love, she thought as she sat in the Denver press box. She wondered if he was thinking about them now, as he stood on the mound studying the Kings' new batter. If the Rebels lost this game the divisional championship and their bid for the pennant would be lost. It was the first time they had come this close to the pennant in five years. But coming close didn't count. All that counted was winning.

Was he thinking about winning, or about her? Or was it all one and the same thing to him? Her old uncertainties returned to haunt her, not as fiercely as before, but they were still there, still waiting to be wrestled with. They refused to die totally.

She scribbled down some notes for her column, but her heart wasn't in it. It was on Ryan. He made love the way he played ball, with determination, but also with control and patience. Did winning her matter? Or would this interlude between them—she refused to call it an affair—ultimately turn out like a ball game, important when it was played, but forgotten as the next one drew near? He had said some wonderful things to her, and he *seemed* sincere, but what if it had only been the heat of the moment that made him say those things? He might be regretting them even now.

Idiot, he has to concentrate on the game, not you, she told herself. If he loses this one they'll hang him.

She knew it didn't help the players' nerves to be playing on someone else's turf. There were Rebel fans in the stands, but the majority of the people were cheering for the Kings.

"Five bucks says the Rebels lose."

Dallas turned to her right. "Don't have much confidence, do you?" she asked the man who had been introduced to her as Harry Vaughn of the *Sun and Times*.

"Do you want to explain that?" The balding man cast a critical eye in her direction. She was the only woman in the press box, and he was of the old school. As far as he was concerned women didn't belong in sports reporting.

"If you did," Dallas explained politely but disdainfully, "you'd bet more than five bucks."

Vaughn considered the source and smiled. Candy from a baby, he thought. "How much you want to bet?"

"Fifty," she shot back without a beat.

"Done."

Ryan wasn't at his best today. She could tell by the way he frowned, by the way he stood. It was her job to know the players' idiosyncrasies, but she was attuned to Ryan in a way she'd never been to any other player before, except for her father. She had always been able to read her father like a book.

Too bad Ryan wasn't in the same league, she thought. Her father had stayed with one team his whole career. Ryan had four to his credit, leaving each as his agent arranged a better deal. His lack of loyalty bothered her, warning her that he might leave her just as easily. And at the bottom of everything was the fact that she felt her father would never have approved of her being in love with a man whose loyalties were transferred so easily, and all because of money.

"Hah! Another run. We're leading!" Vaughn crowed. "Gee, honey," he said, turning to Dallas, "I sure hate taking your money."

"You haven't got it yet." She smiled coolly. "It's not over until both teams are off the field."

He pointed to the scoreboard. There was only one inning remaining. "You believe in miracles?" he asked her.

"No, I believe in Fox."

Harry nudged the reporter next to him, a dark, silent man who hadn't said two words since he entered the box. "They pay her to say that." He chuckled.

Dallas felt her temper rising but told herself it was only the tension of the game that was getting to her. Both games, she corrected. The one on the field and the one in her life.

The Rebels tied the score in the bottom of the ninth, thanks to a double and a sacrifice fly by Rusty. There was still hope, she thought, smugly looking at Vaughn.

The game ran into extra innings. Dallas watched as Gibson marched out to the mound for the third time. She smiled knowingly to herself when she saw Ryan shake his head and Gibson shrug his wide shoulders, palms upturned helplessly toward the gathering clouds in the sky.

They would have to carry Ryan off, she thought proudly. If he didn't have team loyalty, at least he had stamina and pride. She edged her way to the press box door and waved at a passing hot dog vendor.

"Yes, ma'am, what'll it be?"

"One with everything," she said, her eyes trained on the field, afraid she would miss something.

She watched with pride as Ryan faced the Kings.

Dallas held her breath. It was the bottom of the eleventh. He had to hold them off if the Rebels were going to win. How much longer could he go on without tiring?

The Kings sent up their best against him. O'Malley was a powerhouse hitter and rather than try to strike him out, Ryan walked him. And the next man.

"Not such a smart cookie, is he?" Vaughn gloated. "I'll accept a check," he told her obligingly.

"You'll put a lid on it until this is over," Dallas snapped, agonizing for Ryan. If they lost he would carry the blame, even though it was an error on the field that had cost the Rebels two runs. She knew him, knew how his mind worked. He didn't take defeat easily.

An eternity later she felt as if she were drawing her first breath. Ryan struck out the next two players and a pop fly to deep center had taken care of the third. They had won!

"We'll get them tomorrow," Vaughn grumbled as he wrote out a check to Dallas.

She held out her hand expectantly. As he slapped the paper into her hand, she held it up between her fingers. "If this bounces I'll send someone after you," she warned cheerfully. "Thank you. You just bought the winning pitcher dinner." Dallas left as Vaughn was muttering a curse.

She waited outside the locker room, resisting the temptation to go in and throw her arms around him. She was excited, but she didn't want to crowd him. He had said they should to take this one step at a time, and for him right now the most important order of things had to be winning the division, then the league, then the pennant.

And after that? she quizzed herself.

And after that we'll see, she answered.

When Ryan emerged, his hair still damp from his shower, he looked tired. Dallas took his arm, separating him from the reporters who were still dogging his tracks. "Let's go if you don't want to be swallowed up by these vultures." She winked at the nearest man. "Sorry, fellas. I've got an exclusive on this one." She waved her press card over her head as she and Ryan forged out of the area.

"Pretty fair pitching," she said lightly when they reached the outer door.

He could tell how proud she was of him. He could see it in her face. "I kind of thought so," he drawled.

Together they echoed, "Aw, shucks," and laughed.

"Hope you have reservations somewhere, because I'm starved."

"We're going to Rasputin's. It's the nicest place in town," she assured him. "Courtesy of Mr. Harry Vaughn."

"Who's that?"

She dug the check out of her pocket. "A reporter on the *Sun and Times*. The idiot had the nerve to bet me fifty dollars that you couldn't win."

Ryan stopped walking long enough to catch her lips in a searing kiss. "That's what I like in a woman, confidence."

"What else do you like?" She grinned.

"I'll let you know as soon as we're alone," he promised.

But it looked as if they weren't going to be alone for a while. When they walked outside there was a crowd of fans waiting.

"Not nearly as thick as back in L.A.," Dallas commented teasingly, "but it's a healthy showing."

Ryan stayed long enough to sign autographs for them all. Dallas watched, silently marveling at his stamina. He had just pitched eleven innings. Anyone would have excused him if he had just rushed off, yet he stayed until the last fan was satisfied. Maybe, she thought, Pop wouldn't have disapproved of him after all.

"You're really a softie," Dallas said with a laugh when she finally got back exclusive rights to him.

"Shh." He put his finger to his lips. "Don't let the Kings hear you say that."

They hurried to the car she had rented. "What made you stop?" she asked, curious.

He shrugged as he took the keys from her. "I don't know. Maybe it's because when I was a kid I always wanted an autographed ball and never got one."

"There's still a lot of kid left in you." As she said it, she realized that it was true.

"Oh yeah?" he cracked, running his finger along her cheek. "Then that makes you a cradle robber."

"No, I'm talking about baseball, the way you love the game. The smile that lights up your face every time you strike someone out, that's not egotism, or snide satisfaction, that's downright enjoyment."

Did all that go with a man who put money above loyalty? She wasn't certain anymore. She wasn't clear about many of her former beliefs these days. The only thing she knew for certain was that she loved him.

"I like giving my due," he told her. "Remember, I told you that when I join a team they get a hundred percent of me—my concentration, my ability, everything. Or," he continued, starting the car, "they used to."

"And now?"

"Now, whether you like it or not, you've got a piece of the action." The admission cost him less than he had expected. Maybe there wasn't that much pain to this loving business after all. "I had to fight hard out there to forget the way you felt last night in the whirlpool."

"I'm flattered."

"You should be." He guided the car through the tight Friday afternoon traffic. "The last woman I thought about during a game was Alice Ames."

She'd bite. "Was she pretty?"

Ryan chuckled. "She could have stopped a clock."

Dallas was confused. "Then why did you think about her?"

"She was my history teacher. She said she'd flunk me if I didn't get a seventy on the history final. My final was the morning after a big game." He swallowed a curse as a red sports car cut him off.

"And did she?"

"Did she what?"

"Flunk you?"

"No, I got a seventy-one."

"My scholar."

"I did better in other subjects," he informed her, pretending to be defensive.

She was about to say something when she saw that he was turning down the wrong street. "No, you're supposed to make a left at that light."

"I changed my mind." The look in his eyes told her everything. "Let's just call room service. Suddenly my appetite's taken a turn for something more meaningful."

She moved closer and leaned her head on his shoulder. There was something to be said for bench seats, she thought. "I never argue with a winner," she said.

"It wouldn't do you any good, anyway. I'm the one driving."

Yes, she thought, you are. At least for now. Her thoughts turned serious for a second. Was she making a mistake letting him take the driver's seat? She refused to dwell on that. There would be time enough after the end of the series, if the Rebels made it that far, to worry about where her life with him was going, or even if there was a life for them after the series.

She felt her anticipation building as they approached the hotel.

In the lobby they ran into Jawersky, Culhane and Rusty. The next few minutes were spent reliving the game with all its glory and excitement, as if they hadn't already gone over it twice in the locker room. Dallas felt proud as she watched him, but her pride came from association rather than possession; it came from love.

Love, she decided as they stood together in the elevator, his arm possessively around her shoulders, was a frightening thing. You looked for it all your life, and when you found it you wanted to run from it because of all the complications, the pain that was always lurking just out of view. It took a lot of courage to fulfill the responsibilities of loving someone, and she didn't know if she was up to it.

But she was going to make the most of the time she had left to her before the end of the season. There would be time enough for regrets later. Now there was only time for him.

Ryan ordered a simple à la carte meal from room service and wound up autographing a ball for the bellhop who brought their food up.

"Looks like everyone's a baseball fan," he said, removing the lid from one dish.

"It's that time of year. You'll be out in the cold in November." She got up from the sofa and moved toward him with an enigmatic smile on her lips.

He wondered what she was up to. "That's what I like about you, Dallas. You always try to build up my ego."

She wetted her lips with a flick of her tongue. "I intend to." She put her hand over his and lowered the lid back to the plate.

"You don't like Beef Wellington?" he asked.

"Uh-huh." She nodded slowly, her eyes tantalizing him. "But I like you more."

"That's encouraging. Just what do you have in mind?"

"I'm going to make love to you."

"Nope." He crossed his arms in front of his chest as she moved behind him and nibbled on his ear. "*With* me, remember?"

She outlined the rim of his ear with her tongue. He had done things to her, aroused her and turned her emotionally inside out. She wanted to see if she could do the same to him, if she could make him love and desire her as much as she did him. The prospect excited her.

With an effort he twisted around. Dallas put her hands inside his shirt, caressing his skin and making it warm. He saw the mischievous look in her eye. The lady meant business, he thought.

"Be gentle," he teased.

"Sorry." She pretended to be serious. "It's too late for that." Slowly she unbuttoned his pearl-gray shirt, her eyes on his face, weaving their own kind of magic.

Ryan stood perfectly still, wondering how far she would carry this, wondering how long he could endure the pulsating feelings she stirred within him without taking her.

Dallas gently tugged his shirt down his arms, then ran her tongue along his collarbone. She felt him shiver slightly.

"Cold?" she murmured.

"Just the opposite."

"Good."

He raked her sable hair with his hands. "You really are a temptress."

She merely smiled seductively, her breath hot against his chest as her hands caressed his flat stomach, her fingers dipping lower and lower toward his waistband until her hands came to rest at the snap on his jeans. She saw a lazy smile overtake his lips.

"And now what?" he asked.

"We forge ahead," she told him softly. She removed his jeans, guiding them down by placing her hands between the rough material and his smooth, muscular legs. "Step out, please."

"Yes, ma'am," he said as he obeyed.

As she rose he pulled her against him, reveling in the way her body felt against his. He covered her mouth with his lips. For a moment Dallas relinquished her game and let the kiss happen, but then she pushed him away. She couldn't think when he kissed her; she had learned that early on.

"I'm not finished."

"Neither was I," he answered, his voice husky as he struggled for control. He loved this wild, wicked woman in his arms, even though there was a side of her that still troubled him. Even now, while she was driving him wild with desire, he could feel that there was still something coming between them. She still wasn't sure about their being together. What he had with Dallas was special. If only she would let it happen.

The way she was letting this happen now. He drew his breath as her fingers touched him intimately.

"Don't you...think it's about time...you...got rid of your...clothes?" he gasped.

"Not yet."

He wanted to see how she would play this out even while his body screamed its demands. Almost reflexively he pulled her against him as her mouth replaced her hand.

Dallas felt pleasure fill her as Ryan moaned and moved against her. Her own excitement heightened, she began to increase her strokes.

"No," he said hoarsely. He placed his hands on her shoulders and pulled her up to him.

She looked at him, bewildered.

"There's a limit to my control, and in the words of Popeye, 'I can't stands no more.'"

He had her on the bed within an instant, her clothes a thing of the past. His body, hot for the feel of hers beneath him, covered hers in a perfect fit.

Perfect. Everything about this was perfect, she managed to think before all thoughts vanished. But the perfect game soon becomes history, and championship seasons fade. How much would she get to enjoy before she, too, became a thing of the past?

Ryan stopped kissing her and raised himself on his elbows. He touched her temple. "You're thinking again," he accused. "I can feel it."

"What else do you feel?" She moved her body slowly beneath his.

"An incredible need to have you over and over again."

"Better start soon," she urged. "Curfew isn't that far away."

"Neither is heaven," he told her before he covered her mouth with kisses.

The passion that enveloped them eclipsed anything that had taken place before. She marveled at his energy after what he had gone through on the field. She wondered at her own insatiability. He entered her, and she wanted their lovemaking never to stop. Happiness filled her veins, happiness like nothing she had ever experienced.

It wasn't until later, after the tempest of passion had evolved into a breathless peacefulness, that they talked. She lay with her cheek against his chest, her body curled against his, her fingers idly tracing patterns along his abdomen.

He raised her hand to his lips, kissing each finger. "You could get into trouble like that."

She picked her head up, her sable hair falling on his shoulder. "I like trouble like that."

He laughed and hugged her to him as he kissed her forehead. "One more game and we've got the division."

"And then you need four for the pennant and four more for the World Series." She ticked the numbers off on her fingers.

"You don't let up, do you?"

"Never."

He kissed her mouth. "Oh, I forgot to tell you. Dwayne Peterson called me when I got into town."

She cocked her head at the mention of the owner of the Kings. "Was he trying to psych you out?"

"In a way. He said he'd be very interested in discussing my playing for the Kings next season."

She stiffened slightly. "What did you tell him?"

"I said I had a game to win first."

"Did he hang up?" she asked hopefully.

"No, he said that's what he liked about me."

Dallas fell silent. Was he going to move on again? And if he could switch teams so easily after playing so hard with the Rebels, couldn't switching women be just as easy for him, if not easier?

Suddenly Dallas felt lonely again, even in the shelter of his arms.

Eleven

The director of security at Los Angeles Airport had put on ten extra men for the Rebels' homecoming. The players had been alerted before landing, just what was waiting for them below. Southern Californians loved a champion, any champion. Having been accused too often of being laid back, they showed their enthusiasm when their heroes returned home.

And to think, Dallas mused as she deplaned with Ryan and looked around at the crowd, this was only for winning the divisional title. What would it be like when they won the Series?

Won the Series. The words echoed in her head. She smiled to herself. She was a real Rebels fan, all right. She wasn't thinking of "ifs," only "whens."

She spotted a banner being held up by an eager brunette wearing cutoff shorts and a striped tank top. The banner read: I Love You, Ryan.

Dallas nudged him and pointed toward the amply endowed woman. "Friend of yours?"

He turned toward the crowd and saw what had caught Dallas's attention. "Nope. Never saw her before in my life. And in all likelihood I'll never see her again, either."

"Are you sure of that?" Dallas pretended to study him as they walked briskly toward the escalator.

The way he looked at her warmed her. "I'm sure."

"Hey, there's the old man himself," Rusty said as he wedged himself between them.

There, flanked by two very beefy bodyguards and dressed in an inexpensive leisure suit, which utterly belied his wealth, was team owner John H. Jameson, the ex-movie star turned producer turned multimillionaire by grace of a very fortuitous marriage. He smiled broadly, showing off a fortune in dental work as he looked at his team marching through the terminal like tired, triumphant warriors. He had been the one to urge the security director to increase his security force. Jameson didn't want to see any of his players damaged by overzealous fans. No, he wanted "his boys" to be intact for the play-offs next week.

"He looks like a czar welcoming home his army," Dallas commented as they passed the man. She smiled politely and she noticed the nod of approval Jameson gave Ryan.

"With his money, he could be," Ryan said without a trace of envy. "He can buy anything to make the team work. He bought me," he added honestly.

Dallas didn't like the way that sounded, but she swallowed her comment. Instead she asked the question that had been haunting her since he had mentioned Peterson's phone call. "Are you going to tell Jameson about Peterson's offer?"

Several fans broke through the barrier that had been set up by the guards. One managed to reach Ryan, elbowing Dallas out of the way in the process. The girl delivered a very passionate kiss and had to be literally pried away from him by one of the guards.

"Certainly wasn't shy, was she?" Dallas muttered as Ryan hurried her along to the escalator.

Ryan stepped on behind her and gripped the handrail. "You were saying?"

"About the offer . . ." she began hesitantly.

"There isn't an offer yet," he reminded her casually, "Just a hint."

"But there will be," she insisted.

"When he calls with an offer I'll give him an answer."

What answer? she wanted to cry, but didn't. He was interested in playing for the highest salary he could get. Why did that bother her so much? It only made sense. Everyone was doing it, she argued.

But she wasn't in love with everyone, she thought as they made their way out of the terminal, flanked by guards who held the enthusiastic fans at bay. And maybe she just wanted her white knight to shine a little. There wasn't anything quite shiny about a man who kept one eye on his pocket as he pledged his all to his team.

"Why the long face?" Ryan asked as they walked out to the street. More fans circled the entrance to the terminal building waving banners, flags and signs with scrawled messages.

"Just tired," she answered.

He knew there was more to it, but he let it drop. He was too tired himself to wrestle with any problems. He would need all his strength just to get them to his car.

He spent the night at her house. He had only three days of rest before the play-offs started, and he wanted to spend every waking moment with her. Every sleeping one, too.

Dallas slipped out of bed Sunday morning, careful not to wake Ryan. He must really be tired, she thought. He didn't usually sleep this late. Of course, Dallas mused, a three-course dinner and a four-course lovemaking session might have something to do with it.

Her article was going to be in today's paper. She wondered what he would think of it. After shoving her arms into her robe and knotting the sash she went outside. The dewy grass felt cold to her bare feet as she crossed the lawn, looking for the newspaper. It was lying an inch away from the curb.

"That boy will never make a pitcher," she muttered as the hem of her robe flirted with the grass, soaking up dew as she went along.

She pulled out the magazine section and quickly flipped through the pages until she came to her article. They had given her three quarters of page five. At the top was a picture of Ryan, his cap rakishly dipped over his left eye, his grin undoubtedly filtering into a hundred women's fantasies as they drank their morning coffee.

She scanned the article quickly. Satisfied that it had emerged relatively unscathed, she tucked the magazine on top of the paper and marched back into her bedroom.

He was still fast asleep. If only he were as angelic as he looked. If only, she thought, leaning against the doorway and looking at him, he weren't so headstrong. But she wouldn't have wanted a pushover. The relationship wouldn't have clicked the way it did.

Time to put another click into the relationship, she thought, grinning impishly. She dropped the paper on the bed next to him, a corner of one page tickling him on the stomach.

Ryan bolted upright, his left hand held high.

"Down, Fox, you're not pitching now," she laughed.

"Just give me a minute to get my bearings." He ran his hand through his tousled hair. "What are you doing dropping bombs on me this early in the morning?"

"It's not early, and it's not a bomb. It's an article about you. A tad too flattering, probably," she added loftily, "but I wrote it under the influence."

He grinned and pulled her down next to him. The robe opened, and he saw a captivating curve that brought back vivid memories of last night. "I want you right here while I read this. No sneaking out of town." He settled back comfortably against the curve of her body and picked up the magazine section.

"I said it was flattering," she protested.

"I've known a few newspaper people to lie in their time."

"Not me." Her voice was deceptively light.

"No." He stole a quick kiss. "Not you."

"You stole that just like you stole second base during that series against the Kings."

"I like to keep in practice. Now, shh." He deliberately rustled the papers. "I'm reading."

"Sorry." She tried to keep a straight face. "I forgot you're easily distracted."

He stroked her leg as he went on reading. "Only by certain things."

She let him get the gist of the article, estimating when he would be down to the last paragraph. Then she rose on her knees and methodically began to leave a trail of kisses along his collarbone, occasionally taking time out to nip his shoulder.

"Enough," he cried, tossing away the paper. Grabbing her hands, he twisted her around, pinning her against the bed, her hands above her head. Her robe parted provocatively above her waist. "Is there something you wanted?" he asked innocently.

She nodded gravely, her exposed breasts rubbing against his chest.

"What?"

"You."

"I thought you'd never ask."

It was only a good deal later that he finally got around to reading the article carefully. She was good, he thought. Not because of what she said about him, but in the way she wrote. She had a gift, a knack for holding the readers and putting them right into the first row in the stands.

Just like her old man, he thought.

When they had made love earlier he had thought that the barriers between them were almost gone. Almost. The word hung in the air between them as he watched her move around in the kitchen, making him breakfast. She had warned him that she wasn't much of a cook.

He wondered if "almost" would ever be a thing of the past, if she would ever let him fully into her life. He had already decided sometime during the night that she was going to marry him. But he had also decided that she was going to have to come around to the idea on her own. He thought that he would know when that time came.

But he wasn't sure.

He watched as she scorched the pancakes. Well, at least he wasn't going to put on weight after he was married the way a lot of guys did.

Chuckling, Ryan rose to offer his assistance.

It was, Ryan reflected a week and a half later, as if they were playing leapfrog with the other team. The Rebels had taken the first game on their own home field. The Eagles had taken the second. Then they had won the third game at the Eagles' stadium in Pittsburgh, as well as the fifth. In between the Eagles had taken the fourth.

Then, playing back in L.A., the Eagles had won the sixth game in the series, much to the crowd's displeasure. Was it their turn again? Ryan wondered. He had started two of the series games, completing both, but losing one. Was it time to win again?

No, no doubts, he told himself. No doubts and no time to think about the ache in his back or the fact that he could see Dallas watching him from the press box if he looked up. He couldn't afford to think about Dallas now, not until he could go back to her a champion. She expected it, he decided. Her father had been a champion. He had played in five World Series games in his time, and the Rebels had won them all.

Maybe then the barrier between them would finally be gone.

His record thus far this season was impressive. He had gotten 291 strikeouts and had managed, along with breaking the 1912 records for shutouts, to keep up a respectable batting average. For a pitcher .275 wasn't bad. It wasn't bad for any player, he mused, distancing himself from the record, as if all those statistics belonged to another man.

Right now he wished the pressure he was feeling belonged to another man. It was the top of the eighth, and so far he had given up only six hits. "It should've been only three," he muttered, swallowing a curse. The hits had yielded four runs. The Rebels were ahead by one, netted in the bottom of the seventh before a frenzied crowd. But he had to hold the Eagles at bay for another two innings before their own shot at the pennant materialized.

Two more innings. Just one more out in this inning and three more the next, he coached himself. He moved slow and easy, then pitched a fast ball to the Eagles' youngest batter.

Enthusiasm and luck were riding with the batter. He swung hard and caught the ball with the tip of his bat. Rather than sail high and clear, it was a line drive straight toward Ryan. He jumped, but not before the ball clipped him on the right leg. Searing pain shot through his entire nervous system. He went down, aware that Jawersky was flying in from third to snare the ball and throw the player out at first.

Dallas was on her feet along with the rest of the crowd. Her heart was in her throat, beating furiously as she watched Gibson dash out on the field, moving amazingly quickly for a man of his bulk.

Dallas lost no time in getting out of the press box.

"Hey, where are you going?" Mike called after her.

"To see him," she tossed back. But her words were swallowed by the thunderous noise of the crowd.

There had to be a thousand bodies between her and the locker room, she thought. She fought her way through them until she reached the ground level. A security guard blocked her path when she finally made it down from the stands, but she flashed her press pass at him like a sword and ran on.

Was he all right? She hadn't been able to see exactly what had happened. There was no monitor in the box, no instant replay for her to catch. All she knew was that Ryan had crumpled when the ball hit his leg. Was it broken? She shoved her way through the doors.

Dallas heard the sound of his raised voice as she hurried into the locker room. Relieved, she sent up a prayer in thanksgiving.

She elbowed her way through the wall of people surrounding him. She had no idea who they were, nor did she care. The only face she saw clearly was Ryan's. He was sitting on the table, glaring at Gibson.

He sensed her a moment before he saw her. He should have known she would find a way through to him. Having her there only intensified his determination. "There's someone who'll support me," he said, and gestured toward Dallas.

"To the limit," she said mechanically. "What have I just supported?"

"My going back into the game."

Dallas's mouth dropped open. He was hurt! Was he crazy?

"Damn it, Fox, you've been reading your own publicity notices!" she cried. "You're not indestructible and your leg—"

"—is *my* leg." Her attitude surprised him. He had expected her to agree with him. He was doing something she would have expected of her father. He struggled not to let his annoyance show.

"It's not broken?" Dallas asked the team doctor, who was standing at Ryan's left.

"No." The doctor frowned. "But . . ."

"Splint it, tape it, do whatever you have to," Ryan told him. "I want to finish the game."

"Think with your head," Gibson insisted. "You could damage it permanently if you push yourself. What are you going to do, lean on a pair of crutches and pitch?"

"If I need crutches," Ryan retorted, "I'll let you take me out."

"Thank you," came the sarcastic retort. Gibson tugged at his jacket pocket, looking for a cigar that wasn't there.

"Tape it," Ryan repeated, looking at the doctor.

"Ryan, don't you think they're right?" Dallas began. "You're in no condition—"

The look he gave her froze her to the quick. "Only I know what kind of condition I'm in. And I'm going to see this game through. I don't want some relief pitcher buckling under the pressure."

"And you won't buckle?" Dallas shouted angrily. What was the matter with him?

"And I won't buckle," he echoed. He looked down at the man working on his leg. "Well, are you through?"

The doctor withdrew, holding up his hands in surrender. "Try it out," he said patiently. In twenty-three years he had grown used to all sorts of theatrics. But this, he knew, was no play for attention, no attempt at grandstanding. He had only known Ryan Fox for a short time, but Ryan had made an impression on him. He could tell that Ryan really wanted to finish this game, wanted it more than he wanted to walk straight again. Maybe his luck would hold out.

The crowd in the locker room was suddenly quiet as Ryan got off the table and gingerly tested the doctor's handiwork. Dallas didn't know whether to pray that the splint would hold or that the pain would be too great for Ryan to walk.

"Fox?" Gibson asked after a beat.

Ryan took three halting steps and grinned. "I can't square dance, but I can walk."

Dallas saw fresh sweat beading on his forehead. He might be able to walk, she thought, but not without a hell of a lot of pain.

"I can still take you out, you know," Gibson pointed out.

"I know."

It was a simple admission. It was also a plea.

"Damn it, some equal-rights group's probably going to sue me in the morning for inhuman behavior toward injured pitchers. G'wan, get back in the game." Gibson waved him on.

Ryan grinned, relieved. "Thanks, Gib, you won't regret this."

Gibson shook his head and said nothing. Ryan walked past Dallas. "Don't frown, Dallas. I'm planning to come up a winner."

"Good luck, you big idiot."

"That's just what I need." He nodded solemnly. "Old-fashioned encouragement." He walked out ahead of Gibson.

"Never saw such dedication," the doctor muttered, watching the other men leave.

Dallas stood silent for a moment. "I did, once. My dad finished a game with cracked ribs he got while stealing home."

"Oh yes." The doctor nodded, remembering. He had just joined the team himself when that had happened. "That's right, he did. A lot like your dad, isn't he?"

"It looks that way, doesn't it?" Dallas agreed as she walked out.

"So how is he?" Mike asked when Dallas returned to the press box. He noticed that the color had drained from her face.

"He's going to be pitching," she said in a monotone.

"So then he's all right?" Mike pressed.

"No, he's not all right," she snapped. "The idiot won't let the doctor take proper care of his leg until the game's over." Pride and anger mingled in her voice. Ryan had made a decision worthy of her father. She had forgotten just how angry he used to make her when he did things that she thought weren't sensible.

Ryan was acting just like her father had. Even the doctor had seen it. So why was she so upset? It wasn't logical. No, it wasn't, she thought. But she wanted him to be safe more than she wanted him to be a hero.

Maybe that was what real love was all about.

The cheer when Ryan returned to the game was deafening.

Slowly, despite the butterflies in her stomach, Dallas began to smile. That was her man they were cheering. Her knight in shining armor. He had told her that he gave a hundred percent, and he meant to give no less even though he was injured. He was doing just what she wanted him to do. He was showing his loyalty.

She was surprised for a moment when she saw Ryan come up to bat. In all the excitement and tension, she had forgotten that if he were to give up his position in the batting rotation he automatically gave up the mound. He *had* to play.

Dallas almost prayed for him to strike out, afraid of what would happen if he had to run the bases.

So when he connected with the third pitch and sent the ball sailing over the left-field fence, Dallas held her breath waiting for something dreadful to happen as Ryan rounded the bases. It was as if it were all happening in slow motion. She didn't breathe again until he was safe at home plate.

"Now that's what I call grandstanding. First he milks the crowd for sympathy, then he hits a homer. Today that man could write his own ticket," Ashley mused.

No one argued with him, least of all Dallas. Ryan could certainly write his own ticket with her.

And then it was the bottom of the ninth. She watched, nearly breathless, when Ryan slowly walked out on the field as the Eagles readied their last lineup of the day. He would be her hero no matter what the outcome, but would he be his own? she wondered, praying as she never had before.

The first man up had almost a .400 batting average. He was a walking phenomenon with a bat. He would be followed by a known sacrifice player, then another strong hitter, topped off by a cleanup batter who theoretically would drive a grand slam over the fence and send everyone home.

Theoretically. But theory and practice were a long way apart, especially when faced with almost superhuman determination.

The first two strikeouts happened so fast that Dallas thought the game was in the bag. But the third batter walked, and then the fourth batter came under a full count, three balls and two strikes. Was Ryan tiring? Dallas wondered, aching for him. She could almost feel every movement he made in her own body. She sat on the edge of her seat, watching, a tiger set to spring. No one spoke in the box. All eyes were on Ryan and the so-called cleanup batter. If he hit a home run the game, the play-off and the future belonged to the Eagles.

Ryan stood on the mound. The ache in his leg was incredible, and the pain was making him progressively weaker. But at the same time it was almost as if all this were happening to someone else. He distanced himself from the field, from the heat, the noise, the expectant crowd.

Millhouse was waiting for a slider, Ryan judged. After all, it was his speciality.

Slowly the pitch came. It was a change-up, floating toward home plate at nearly half the speed of the 90 mile-per-hour fastball the batter had been expecting. Millhouse swung, tying himself in knots trying to hold back.

He missed.

It was over!

Ryan was carried off the field, perched high on the shoulders of his teammates, the joyous screams of the fans echoing in his ears.

Twelve

Dallas saw pure madness sweep over the fans in the stadium. It had a life and a texture all its own. People all around her fell victim to it. It was as if each person in the stands had personally won the championship. Kinship swept over one and all as strangers hugged, laughed and detailed plays for one another.

The press box itself was full of noise and awed speculation as to whether or not Ryan would be in shape for the World Series. Dallas had no doubts in her mind. He would be, come hell or high water. She knew that now. She had seen the look of determination in his eyes, and that, she realized, was the ultimate test of loyalty.

She took her time getting to the locker room. The celebration within would have gotten underway immediately, with bottles of champagne used to drench the players, creating foamy rivers along the locker room floor.

"Hi, Gilhooley," Dallas said, seeing a familiar face outside the locker room.

The old guard grinned at her. "Some game, eh?"

"Some game," she echoed as she pushed open the door.

The word *bedlam* was hardly adequate to describe the scene that greeted her. Grown men were in the process of releasing the tension that had filled them for over a week. The noise was deafening as everyone tried to be heard over everyone else. Reporters were everywhere, saving the celebration for posterity.

Someone grabbed her waist, and she felt herself being spun around. Before she could focus in on her captor she was being soundly kissed.

"I've been wanting to do that for a long time," Jawersky said, releasing her. "Figured I'm allowed, since I bailed The Fox out."

Yes he was. He had been there when Ryan needed him. "After that play at the top of the ninth you're entitled," she told him.

He cupped his ear, unable to make out her words clearly because of the noise. "What? Ryan? Oh, he's over there," Jawersky shouted, pointing behind him.

Ryan sat on the table, slightly removed from the others. His injury had earned him a place by himself, although it hadn't exempted him from being doused with champagne. Rusty had taken care of that, emptying an entire bottle of California's best over the winning pitcher's head.

When he saw Dallas, Ryan reached out toward her, and she quickly joined him.

She kissed him and ran her tongue along his cheek. "Hmm, I like my champagne salty."

"I'll try to remember that." He rested his right hand easily on her hip. It was a natural gesture, and it spoke volumes to his teammates.

She hooked her arm around his shoulders. "You're a big idiot, you know that?"

"Why, because I love you?" he asked innocently.

"No, because—" She shook her head as if to clear it. It had to be the noise. "What did you say?"

"I said I love you."

She looked into his smoky eyes. He wasn't kidding. "I'm canceling the big-idiot speech."

"I thought you might." His strong fingers grasped her waist, and he kissed her long and hard. It took a moment for them to realize that they had suddenly become the center of attention, augmented by wolf calls, cheers and clapping. As they separated slightly Dallas noticed that their brief moment had also been saved on film.

Goes with the territory, she thought philosophically.

"Are you going to have that looked at?" a reporter asked, pushing a microphone up between them and waving at Ryan's bandaged leg.

No, she thought, annoyed at the stupid question. He's going to hobble around for the rest of his life. "As a matter of fact," Dallas said loudly, "he was just about to do that." She looked at Ryan pointedly. "The car's ready."

"So am I." It was time to leave the center of the whirlwind and be alone with her. He had earned the right. Ryan eased himself off the table and this time allowed a grimace to pass over his face.

"Want to lean on me?"

"Only if you'll do the same."

She understood what he meant. "We can negotiate."

The word brought back an unsettled question as they made their way out again. Was he going to call the Kings' owner and talk about a contract? She knew she wanted him to turn down any other offers. She wanted him to stay with the Rebels. She had decided that she wanted the icing on the proverbial cake. While following the team during the season, she would be with him all the time. In the winter months she would mind the home bench and cover the general sport desk, letting the other reporters go on the road. It would work out perfectly.

The sea of people in the locker room parted as Ryan and Dallas walked slowly toward the door. There were shouts of encouragement to Ryan, telling him that all would be fine with his leg and his lady friend.

Dallas saw Rusty, who gave her the high sign as well as a wide grin. The next minute someone was dumping a magnum of champagne over him. He turned up his face and drank all he could catch in his mouth.

"I thought we'd drive down to Marina Hospital," Dallas told Ryan once they made it out the locker room doors.

"Hospital beds aren't all that comfortable for what I have in mind."

"Comfort is usually the last thing involved for what you have in mind," she said, thinking of the whirlpool. She looked around for Gilhooley, but the guard was gone. Down the corridor, she saw another guard. She waved at him, and he walked over to them, looking at Ryan with the respect due to a conquering champion.

"I want to get this man to a hospital," she told the guard. "Will you run interference for us?"

The guard did his best to get them out to the parking lot, but insistent fans waving autograph books blocked their way. It took them forty-five minutes to get to the car.

"At this rate your leg will mend on its own," Dallas muttered, trying not to show how worried she was about him.

"Good, because I have no intention of going to a hospital." He eased himself into the passenger seat.

Dallas shut the door and went around to the driver's side. "Ryan," she said impatiently.

"Dallas," he said in the same voice.

She wasn't going to be baited. "Look, this is no laughing matter." She looked accusingly at his leg.

"Dallas, the doctor took another look at it before Rusty gave me my champagne bath. He says it'll be fine in time for my first Series game."

She shot him an annoyed look, then stomped on the gas. "This time I'm driving and we go where I say."

He shook his head, resigning himself to the inevitable. "Just plain headstrong."

"You should talk," she countered.

He shrugged, slumping down in his seat. "I'm too tired to argue."

"You wouldn't win anyway."

She thought she heard him laugh softly.

She took him to the emergency room, where the admitting nurse gaped when she saw Ryan come in leaning on Dallas's shoulder.

"I think we just ran into another fan," Dallas muttered under her breath.

The woman blushed as she pointed to a seat at the desk. She barely looked down at the form as she wrote. It took a moment for her to collect herself and tell them that it would be a few minutes before someone would come to see him.

"Hah," Ryan said to Dallas as he rose. "I know better. I've known people who've grown old and died in emergency rooms before they were called."

Dallas watched the nurse dash into the back. She was probably going to tell everyone who was out in the waiting room, Dallas surmised.

"I wouldn't get too comfortable if I were you," Dallas said as Ryan began lowering himself into a seat.

"From the looks of that nurse they're going to be wheeling you in there posthaste. People like to look at stars."

"Why are you putting me through this?" he muttered, shaking his head.

"Because..." The words trembled on her lips and then she freed them. "Because I love you."

He smiled. "I can accept that."

"I'm afraid you have no choice," she answered. And neither, she thought, do I. She rolled the thought over in her mind, getting comfortable with it for the first time. Maybe things would work out at that.

True to Dallas's guess, Ryan was taken in to be examined within five minutes, ahead of several other patients who were waiting. No one seemed to mind.

"Glory has its rewards," Ryan muttered, hobbling behind a nurse.

"Just don't let it go to your head," Dallas called after him. And then she sat down to wait.

She waited for what seemed like forever. The magazines she flipped through didn't begin to hold her attention. She couldn't shake the feeling that he had done something terrible to himself by insisting on going back into the game. Then she upbraided herself for being stupid. Could he have stood all that time, pitching, if the leg had really been damaged?

By the time Ryan returned her nerves were just about at the breaking point. "Well?" she demanded.

He opened his mouth to answer when another technician burst through the doors. He had a baseball in his hand. "I found it!" the man cried triumphantly.

"Excuse me," Ryan said to Dallas. She could have sworn he was enjoying prolonging her agony. "My public is calling."

She waited until he finished signing. "The coroner will be calling if you don't answer me," she said between gritted teeth. "Is there any damage?"

"Only to my heart."

Dallas tried again. "Then you're all right?"

"Only if a certain sexy sports reporter will minister to me with tender loving care." He put an arm around her shoulders and steered her to the exit.

"Okay," Dallas said gamely, watching him get into the car, "so where do you want to go?"

He tried to get comfortable and gave up. "Your place."

"My place it is."

She headed north. "You are all right, aren't you?"

"Except for the fact that I'm jammed into an undersized car, yes. It's just a hell of a bruise. I was damn lucky." He tapped his leg twice.

She nodded. Several minutes passed in silence. She knew she had a lot to be grateful for, to be content with, but she *had* to ask. "Ryan?"

He was leaning back in the bucket seat, toying with a strand of her hair. "Hmm?"

"Have you given any thought to the Kings' offer?" She tried to sound nonchalant, but she knew she wasn't fooling him. He had grown to know her too well. There were people out there who had known her all her life and didn't know half as much about her as he had learned in only a few short weeks. Insight and sensitivity counted for something, didn't they? she asked herself.

"That's really bothering you, isn't it?"

She heard the playfulness leave his voice, replaced with something akin to disappointment.

"Yes."

"Why?"

She licked her lips. "I'm afraid you'll leave the team."

"Oh, so that's it. We're back to the image of me as a mercenary, aren't we?" There was an edge in his voice. After all they had been through it annoyed him that she should take this stand.

"No," she denied, surprised at his accusation. "Not after what I saw this afternoon. They don't pay you extra for standing up in pain."

The tension drained from his body. "What pain?" he said glibly.

Without her realizing it, her foot was all the way down on the accelerator, the speed of the car mirroring her annoyance. "Don't give me that. You're not Superman." Did he believe his own press releases?

"But I've been competing with one."

His quiet words completely threw her. "What?"

"Your father."

She took the long narrow lane that led to her house. "What's my father got to do with this?"

"Everything. You've measured everything I've done against the image you have of him in your head." He worked hard to check the bitterness he felt. "Now I'll be the first to admit he was a legend in his own time— a legend for all time, actually—but it gets kind of hard on a man to compete with a legend."

They reached her house, and she stopped the car, staring at him dumbfounded. "I wasn't comparing you." Even as she denied it, she realized he was right. She *had* been comparing them because she wanted someone as perfect as she remembered her father to be, someone out of her past, when everything had been right. She'd been an idiot. The past was just that, the past. And nothing had ever been perfect.

"Oh, yes, you were. Every step of the way."

She watched him get out of the car without making a move of her own.

"Are you coming?" he asked.

"It's my house." Numbly she followed, fishing out her key. "Is that why you finished out the game?"

"No," he snapped, then relented. "Maybe in part. But I did it because I do feel a commitment. Just because things are different now than they were back when your dad was a star doesn't mean that they're necessarily bad. Just different," he repeated.

She opened the door, and they walked inside in silence. His words rang in her ears. She tried to deny them, then found she couldn't. What he'd said was true. Hadn't she felt it? Hadn't that been the reason she had panicked at first? Fear of change was what had made her seek a different outlet for her work in the first place. She didn't like the changes that were happening to baseball, didn't like the way they intruded on her memories of the past. And she needed the past, because that was when she had felt loved, when she had felt a part of someone.

She turned to look at Ryan. He had taken the same seat on the sofa where he had been the first night they made love.

"You look like you're settling in," she said.

"That's up to you."

She sat down beside him on the floor, resting her head against his good knee. She gave him her answer in her own way. "Won't Gibson be upset about you breaking training? After all, there is still the Series to face."

"Gib'll understand," he said softly, tangling his fingers in her hair.

"Why? Because you played ball under duress and won?" Her words came unhurriedly as she gave herself up to the feelings that were beginning to rise within her.

"No, because I'm proposing and being accepted."

Dallas raised her head. She stared at him in disbelief.

"I *am* being accepted, aren't I?"

"I don't know," she said, her throat dry. "What is it you're proposing?"

"Marriage," he said softly. "I can't promise you a championship season, but I can promise you me. Now, what do I tell Gibson?"

She rose to her knees, her mouth covering his, and tasted the sweet, tempting flavor of his lips. "Tell him I accept, but I want a clause in my contract that says I can't be traded."

His arms enfolded her. "Not for any amount," he promised. "And for the record, I've decided to stay with the Rebels." He thought her grin would split her face.

"What made up your mind?"

"I like the reporter the *L.A. News* assigned to follow us around."

"Good taste." She nodded.

"I always said that." He kissed her again, knowing this time that things would be all right. "Oh, by the way, I thought of asking Rusty to be best man."

She shook her head, linking her arms around his neck. "He can't be."

"Why not?" He had thought she would have picked Rusty herself.

"Because you are."

He could find no argument with that as he took her into his arms again.

ATTRACTIVE, SPACE SAVING BOOK RACK

Display your most prized novels on this handsome and sturdy book rack. The hand-rubbed walnut finish will blend into your library decor with quiet elegance, providing a practical organizer for your favorite hard-or soft-covered books.

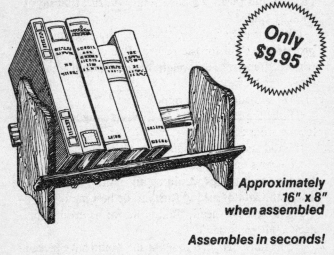

Only $9.95

Approximately 16" x 8" when assembled

Assembles in seconds!

To order, rush your name, address and zip code, along with a check or money order for $10.70 ($9.95 plus 75¢ postage and handling) (New York residents add appropriate sales tax), payable to *Silhouette Reader Service* to:

In the U.S.

Silhouette Reader Service
Book Rack Offer
901 Fuhrmann Blvd.
P.O. Box 1325
Buffalo, NY 14269-1325

Offer not available in Canada.

BKR-2

Silhouette Intimate Moments
Love stories that entice;
longer, more sensuous romances
filled with adventure,
suspense, glamour
and melodrama.
NOW AVAILABLE IN CANADA
SIL-IM-1A